He drew his gun, go in first.

When all was clear, he headed for the stairway. With any luck he'd tell Gemma good-night and retire to his guest room, alone. But when he turned the corner, they collided. She lost her balance with a small, startled sound, flailing her arms. Catching her around the waist, he stepped down two of the stairs to keep them both from falling.

Her hands came against his biceps and her soft brown eyes peered up at his, her lips parted with surprise. She slid her hands up his arms to his shoulders, enough of an invitation for him.

He leaned down to kiss her.

She parted her lips, encouraging him more....

Dear Reader,

What a pleasure contributing to this perfect continuity! Full of action and suspense, each book in the series offers a great getaway to a land of paradise gone awry. I hope you'll find *Lawman's Perfect Surrender* a perfect addition to the series!

My favorite parts in the writing of this story are the main characters. This continuity is full of fascinating people who enrich the town's elite and bountiful facade. Gemma Johnson has spice for life and newfound optimism after escaping an abusive ex-husband. And Ford McCall is the perfect man for her. Haunted by a tragic past, he's driven to uphold the law. What's hard for them both is trusting enough to relax their defenses after enduring so much pain.

Writing their characters was a satisfying exploration of courage and the invincible power of love. May you feel the emotion as the two grow together.

Happy reading,

Jennifer Morey

Watch out for these titles in the Perfect, Wyoming miniseries:

Special Agent's Perfect Cover by Marie Ferrarella—January 2012
Rancher's Perfect Baby Rescue by Linda Conrad—February 2012
A Daughter's Perfect Secret by Kimberly Van Meter—March 2012
The Perfect Outsider by Loreth Anne White—May 2012
Mercenary's Perfect Mission by Carla Cassidy—June 2012

JENNIFER MOREY

Lawman's Perfect
Surrender

ROMANTIC

SUSPENSE

Special thanks and acknowledgment to Jennifer Morey for her contribution to the Perfect, Wyoming miniseries.

Recycling programs
for this product may
not exist in your area.

ISBN-13: 978-0-373-27770-4

LAWMAN'S PERFECT SURRENDER

www.Harlequin.com

Printed in U.S.A.

Books by Jennifer Morey

Harlequin Romantic Suspense

Special Ops Affair #1653
Seducing the Accomplice #1657
Lawman's Perfect Surrender #1700

Silhouette Romantic Suspense

The Secret Soldier #1526
Heiress Under Fire #1578
Blackout at Christmas #1583
"Kiss Me on Christmas"
Unmasking the Mercenary #1606
The Librarian's Secret Scandal #1624

*All McQueen's Men

Other titles by this author available in ebook format.

JENNIFER MOREY

Two-time 2009 RITA® Award nominee and a Golden Quill winner for Best First Book for *The Secret Soldier,* Jennifer Morey writes contemporary romance and romantic suspense. Project manager du jour, she works for the space systems segment of a satellite imagery and information company and lives in sunny Denver, Colorado. She can be reached through her website, www.jennifermorey.com, and on Facebook—jmorey2009@gmail.com.

To Sandra Long, ex-detective for the Boulder, Colorado, Sheriff's Department, for helping me with crime scene investigations. Her knowledge and advice were invaluable to me when writing this story.

Laura Leonard and Susan LeDoux—the best proofreaders I could ask for!

Jackie, my adorable twin,
I wish everyone knew you the way I do.

My homey. Thanks for doing things like watching movies with your daughter in the Jeep while I attend R-rated book readings. No man I've ever met compares.

And as always, Mom.

Chapter 1

After talking to the fire chief about final plans for this week's Fourth of July celebration, Ford McCall tucked his cell phone into its holster and looked with dread toward the front doors of Samuel Grayson's lavish three-story community center. Marble-trimmed, tinted windows and swooping gardens full of color accented the stone monolith. This was Inspiration Central at its finest, cloaked in danger and deception. The whole town was infected with its cultish poison.

Ford sighed and ran his fingers through his windblown blond hair, annoyed that he had to deal with another woman who'd caught Grayson's fancy. The Chief of Police had assigned him to question a "very special lady." She was special, all right. Grayson always took an interest in anything that put a ripple in his perfect town, and he used the police chief to take care of the problem. Gemma Johnson had moved here after divorcing her ex-husband, Jed, who hadn't taken her leaving well and found and beat her. Now she was scared and vulnerable.

She must be vulnerable. Otherwise, Ford would not have found her here, attending one of Grayson's early-evening, soul-perfecting seminars.

With the summer sun low in a clear blue sky, the doors to the Cold Plains Community Center opened and a throng began to emerge. He spotted her almost immediately. She wore white cropped pants with a dark blue-and-white sleeveless blouse. All he'd seen of her was a picture, but it was enough. She walked slowly beside the taller Lacy Matthews, the owner of the posh and trendy Cold Plains Coffee.

The two must have struck up a friendship, thanks to the seminars. Another bad sign for the newcomer. Lacy was well on her way to no return. Ford wouldn't be at all surprised if she already had a *D* for *Devotee* tattooed on her hip. Grayson liked to brand his truest followers that way. If Gemma wasn't careful, she'd be drawn into his secret tattoo parlor just like the others.

As the women drew closer, Ford couldn't help noticing Gemma in a very different light from the one that brought him here. Small-boned, almost fragile, she had a tiny waist, slender hips and breasts a little larger than a handful. Lean and sexy. Though her lower lip and nose were still swollen and the cuts and bruises on her face were still clearly visible, he could see she was a beautiful woman. Silky dark hair waved gently as she moved and she had the softest brown eyes he'd ever seen.

Putting a stop to his wandering fascination, he circled back to his purpose here. His job was to question her about her ex-husband and then find and arrest him, not ask her out on a date.

The first of the attendees to leave the building passed. Some greeted him warmly, others looked over in suspicion. Why was Police Deputy Ford McCall dressed in uniform and standing beside his flashy, department-issued Escalade, in front of Samuel Grayson's community center? Was he waiting? Who was he waiting for? Ford found it ironic that no one batted an eye over the higher-ranking officers driving such pricey vehicles. This was Cold Plains, the city where beauty and prosperity thrived. It was only natural that city officials suited the culture while they worked to keep the town safe. If the Chief of Police, Bo Fargo, wanted to spend that kind of money, who was Ford to complain? He was more concerned with the unsolved murders and mysteriously disappearing residents, all occurring in the time frame Samuel Grayson had been here.

"Ms. Johnson?" he called when Lacy and Gemma were about to pass.

Gemma stopped, and so did Lacy.

The seminar attendees who'd heard him paused with curiosity. An older woman ornamented with diamonds smiled her approval. *The police are doing their job,* he could almost hear her thinking. Gemma had obviously been accosted, therefore, justice needed to be done. Someone had to purge the town of the thug who'd done it. Clean out the trash, as it were. Grayson would love that. But his reasons were different than Ford's. Much different.

"Gemma Johnson?" he said to the woman's stunned face.

Stepping closer, he saw that he towered over her small frame as she gazed up at him with those lovely, uncertain, flighty eyes.

"Deputy McCall, Cold Plains Police. I'd like to talk to you about Jed Johnson. Is now a good time?"

After blanching slightly, she stammered, "O-oh...I—I... of course."

Ford turned to Lacy. "Ms. Matthews."

Lacy bowed her head congenially. "Deputy McCall." Then she turned to Gemma. "Stop by Cold Plains Coffee tomorrow morning. I'll make you a vanilla latte and we can talk more."

Gemma's smile was big, tripping Ford up with its dazzling warmth. "I'd love that."

She'd fallen so easily into Lacy's magnetic personality. Or was it the smile itself that had grabbed him? Yes. It was the smile. Beautiful. Guileless. Full of innocent delight. Wide, white and toothy. It lit up her face and wiped away all the vulnerability and fear.

Lacy walked away.

Given Ford's suspicion of Lacy's affiliation with Grayson, he didn't trust Gemma's friendship with her. Lacy had her priorities, and they centered around Grayson.

That smile transfixed him all over again, now softening as she regarded him. The way it made him feel reminded him too much of the past, back when initial sparks led to heartache. He briefly glanced away, only to catch another seminar attendee eyeing them speculatively.

"Would you like to go somewhere to talk?" he asked her.

"Oh…" She glanced across the street to a brick diner with a bright green sign that said Fleur de Sel's. It was immaculately clean and modern.

"All right. Yes."

He offered his arm to her and she looped hers through it, leaning a little of her weight against him. She'd be sore for a while but she'd recover. He helped her across the street and they entered the French diner beneath several curious gazes. It was getting late in the evening so there were a few tables open. Unfortunately, most of the patrons had come from the community center.

After Ford asked for a booth along the front windows, the hostess led them there. He wanted something relatively private. Sitting across from Gemma, he pulled out a pen and a little notebook.

"Have you ever been here before?" she asked.

Realizing she was referring to the restaurant, he answered, "No."

"It's very good. I like to find the best, and this is definitely one of those."

He didn't really care about that. But he suspected she was only nervous. "Why don't we start with what happened?" She'd have to face it sometime.

Her eyes lowered to the table. "How did you find out? I didn't call the cops."

A waitress appeared, interrupting them.

"Are you hungry?" he asked.

"No. Lacy and I had dinner before the seminar." She looked up at the waitress. "Just water for me." And then to Ford she said, "They do have a chocolate croissant here that stands apart from all others. You should try it for breakfast some time. It's really good. The best."

"Everything is in this town," he quipped, only half kidding, then to the waitress, "Just black coffee for me."

The tall and slender, beautifully groomed woman in a green apron embroidered with a Fleur de Sel logo snapped her order book shut and turned away.

Gemma's nervousness eased and she smiled at his sarcasm. He grinned back at her and offered no explanation.

Relaxing even more, she settled back against the bench seat and studied him as though trying to figure him out on her own. Her gaze fell down over his chest, spending more time on his badge before rising again. Her light brown eyes sparkled with health and vitality, and the same fascination that had overcome him. None of the frailty he'd sensed when he'd first announced he wanted to talk to her about Jed remained. The change in her was magnificent. And she was so beautiful he couldn't stop staring at her. The more he stared, the more he wanted to make Jed pay for marking her with cuts and bruises.

Suddenly aware of the heat that had risen out of nowhere, he reeled it in. The quicksilver reaction came without welcome. She'd struck him right away, at first sight. That was unusual. When a woman caught his eye, he normally had time to assimilate whether he wanted to pursue her. With

Gemma, it slam-dunked him, thrust him right in the middle of an unexpected attraction.

Not understanding why she did that to him, he tapped his pen on the notebook. "The Chief of Police told me to come get your statement."

As he'd hoped, her demeanor cooled.

"That's how I know your ex-husband came after you," he answered her previous question. He didn't tell her that Doctor Rafe Black had also spoken to him, voicing his concern over Grayson's interest in her after he'd treated her at the hospital.

"Ah." She nodded and averted her gaze.

"Would you mind telling me exactly what happened?"

She glanced at him and then down at the table again, the vulnerability he'd noticed before returning. He could understand how this would be hard for her.

"Did he break into your home?" he helped her out.

She lifted her eyes. "No. I—I left the back door open. I know I should have locked all my doors, but I'd been feeling so safe here. He walked right in."

Lots of people felt safe and secure here…at first. He could tell she felt like a fool for that and hoped it had shown her not to trust her impression of Cold Plains as an idyllic town. It was, but not with Samuel Grayson in it.

"You were surprised to see him?" he asked.

"Oh, yeah." She nodded a few times. "He was really angry. He sent me a few emails before coming to find me. I ignored them all, of course. He wanted to reconcile and I wasn't about to do that. The divorce was already final and I've moved on. When he came here, he kept asking me if I thought I could just walk away from him. I told him to leave or I'd call the police and then he…that's when he attacked me. He hit me and kicked me until I thought I was going to die. He broke my Tiffany lamp when he threw it at me and it hit the wall. I *loved* that lamp." She pouted.

She sounded more upset over the lamp than being attacked. Did she favor material things or was the lamp something special to her? "You fought him off?"

"No. I mean, yes, I fought him, but he stopped beating me and said he'd be back and I could either go with him or he'd kill me. It's like he was giving me time to think about it." She shook her head incredulously. "I thought he was going to kill me then, but he only wanted to warn me."

Ford finished jotting down some notes. "So he said he'd be back for you. Did he say when?"

"No." She took a deep breath and looked away.

"Do you have any pictures of him?"

"No. I burned them all."

"I should be able to come up with something. Can you describe him for me?"

"He's tall." She surveyed him. "Not as tall as you. He might be as big but he's not as...fit."

Every man probably seemed big to her, as tiny as she was.

"Dark hair. Hazel eyes." She shuddered.

Clearly she didn't like his eyes. They probably scared her.

"He wore jeans and one of his Armani Collezioni dress shirts. It was dark blue. He always spent a lot of money on his clothes. He hoarded his money for them, even though he had plenty for both of us to shop like that. He was furious if I ever spent money on anything other than clothes I needed to be seen with him in public. He made me go to consignment stores, where I'd find used brand names. He kept me from seeing my friends and never let me out of his sight except when he went to work, and even then he checked on me constantly to make sure I didn't go anywhere. It's a miracle he didn't feed me dog food."

Ford had to stifle a chuckle. The tone of her voice told him how much she hadn't liked the way her ex-husband had treated her, but she was able to inject some humor into it. Jed had lavished himself with luxurious items and forced her to cut corners. Was that why material things were important to her? No one was going to stop her from doing what she wanted now? From spending money the way she wanted to? He liked the hint of rebellion in her. Innocent rebellion. She could have decided to run a key down the side of her ex's car, but instead she treated herself to shopping sprees. Bo had told him she'd come to town with money, her ex-husband's money. Her money now.

The waitress returned with the coffee and water. He put down his pen to sip, seeing Gemma do the same.

"Bo said Jed followed you here."

She lowered her glass and answered solemnly, "Yes."

"Where did he come from?"

"Casper, Wyoming." She provided an address, putting her elbows on the table.

"How long were you married?"

"Not long. Three years."

"Did he beat you before this incident?"

"Yes. It started around the first year of our marriage. By the end of that last year it got really bad. At first he didn't get physical very often and he always apologized. I think he genuinely was sorry and just couldn't help himself, you know? It gradually got worse." She shook her head in disgust and slipped her hands down to her lap. "This time was worse than ever, though. I had never required a doctor until now."

"How did he find you? Did you tell him where you were going?"

"No. No way. I don't know…he probably found out through my old job." She rubbed her hands on her pants, which fitted her body perfectly, he recalled.

"We'll get a restraining order going, and I'll arrange for some scheduled patrols to watch your house."

Smiling her appreciation, she stopped nervously rubbing her pants. Her smile derailed his train of thought again.

"Samuel said you would," she said, snapping him out of his trance.

"Really? He said I would?"

"No, I mean he said the police would."

The fondness in her voice didn't go unnoticed. "How did he find out?"

"I don't know. He came to the hospital to see how I was doing. He was very nice."

That's what he wanted everyone to believe. But Grayson was anything but nice.

Ford was onto Grayson and his cult. Only the FBI team sent to investigate him knew how much attention he was giving to five murders and the mysterious disappearances of people who once lived here. They'd all occurred after Grayson had arrived. He was very good at escaping incrimination. He had a network of henchmen and followers and never left any trails. In order for Bo to protect Samuel, he needed Ford, a figure of law-abiding goodness in the department.

Ford would let him keep thinking he could use him like that. So far it had worked in his favor. He wouldn't tell Gemma anything she could reveal to either Bo or Samuel that would jeopardize that. But there was one thing he meant to find out from her.

Taking the bill from the waitress, he gave it back to her with his debit card.

"Are you close to Samuel Grayson?" he asked Gemma.

"I wouldn't say close. He's shown me a lot of kindness and I love what he does for this town. And for me."

"What has he done for you?"

Taking a moment to think, she finally said, "Made me feel stronger. And safe." Her fond expression warmed even more. "He sent me you."

Ford withheld a sarcastic remark. Samuel ran the town, and as long as no one crossed him no one disappeared. There was nothing to love about him or his motives. He was good at fooling people. Especially newcomers. And vulnerable women like Gemma.

"You attend his seminars on a regular basis?" he asked.

Once again, her megawatt smile threw him off balance. "Oh, yes! They're *so* wonderful. Samuel is *such* a great speaker. He's helped me heal after all I've gone through. I don't know what I would have done without him, without the seminars. They're exactly what I need right now."

He smiled back, wishing she was praising anything other than Grayson and those mind-warping seminars.

"Samuel is an incredible man. He's a visionary. Inspirational, and…a real beacon of hope."

Ford could believe that, given her history of abuse. Any kind of encouragement would soak into her like water into a paper towel.

"Have you gone to any of them?" she asked, still dreamy-eyed.

He couldn't stop a cynical chuckle. The idea of going to any of the sessions was comical. "No."

At the sound of his bold voice, she angled her head and a coy look entered her eyes. "Would it threaten your manhood?"

"No." He shook his head. Not even close.

"Then why don't you go?"

"I don't need them," he answered simply.

His reply only seemed to feed her coyness, which he was reluctant to call infatuation. "You're already the best man you can be?"

"If that's the way you want to look at it, yes."

"I like a man who's sure of himself."

He liked a woman who smiled the way she did. He looked at her straight white teeth and the light of happiness sparkling in her beautiful eyes. After all she'd been through, she still had a sunny side. And a strong side, too. He doubted those seminars had anything to do with that. It was natural, something that had already been there, had been awakened with a little encouragement. She met his gaze and they fell into a long stare that he began to feel too much.

The waitress returned with his card and receipt and he was glad to add the tip and be done with this.

Standing, he tucked the pen and notebook into his shirt pocket. "That's enough for now. I'll call you if anything comes up."

"Okay." She seemed awkward now, as if she'd noticed the change in him.

She led him out the front door and he helped her to her car in the community-center parking lot.

"Are you okay to drive?" he asked.

"Oh, yes. I'm better now, other than a few cuts and bruises."

He nodded once and handed her his business card. "Just in case."

She smiled, but not as brightly as before, and took the card. "Thanks." He wondered if she was disappointed because she thought he wasn't interested. He was, and that was the problem. Not only was he on duty, falling in love wasn't his thing. Not that he'd fall in love with Gemma. He didn't even welcome the possibility to present itself. Maybe when he was older…years from now. One round of that was enough to keep him casual for a while, and Gemma didn't strike him as the casual type.

As he watched her drive away, he noticed a boy sitting on a motorcycle who looked familiar. He was parked in a space that was partially concealed by a tree and shrubs and seemed to be watching the entrance to the center. Tall and lean, he wore a helmet that hid shaggy black hair and a Ryan Gosling face.

Ford followed his look and saw Grayson emerge with a couple in their early fifties. Mr. and Mrs. Monroe. Two of Grayson's Devotees? Curtis Monroe seemed to be. His wife appeared rather bored.

Looking back at the boy, he finally placed him. Dillon was the couple's teenaged son. The boy spotted him and started the motorcycle, glancing once more at his parents before motoring away. Why had he been watching the community center?

Ford turned back to Grayson, who waved as the couple headed for the parking lot. Then Grayson saw Ford and waved again in greeting.

Ford saluted him, turning toward his Escalade. Some day the man would be behind bars. And he was going to do everything he could to help put him there.

He probably thought she was stupid. *You're already the best man you can be?* Had she actually said that? Gemma stopped her brand-new red Charger in her gravel driveway where a cement path led to the front door of her house.

She had no plans to find a boyfriend. Yet, meeting Ford had her flirting without reservation. It had come naturally. She hadn't even thought to hold back the impulse. Impulse had led her to marry Jed and look where that had gotten her. She had to learn to use her head with men. Jed had shown her that not every man could be trusted.

Maybe Ford made her feel safe and that's why she'd lost her head. He was a cop. A handsome cop. Seeing him standing outside the community center in front of his big black Escalade had given her the impression of ominous power. He hadn't disappointed close up, either. His blue eyes had riveted her. His wind-tousled blond hair made her imagine running her fingers through the thick, healthy strands. His height and muscular build only added to his general aura of indomitable strength and resolve. Sureness built from experience. And then there was the uniform. Something about it fascinated her. He was a lawman. A representation of everything Jed wasn't.

Ford's effect on her still lingered, warm and mysterious.

Jed had made her feel things, too. Things that had turned out to be false. Just because Ford was a cop didn't mean she could throw her heart at him and trust him to take care of it. She had to stop jumping into relationships that way. Heart first.

Getting out of her car and pressing the lock button on her fob, she walked toward the front door of the old house she'd bought. She glanced around to make sure Jed didn't pop out of the fading light. The sun had sunk beyond the horizon but the sky still held a blue hue, casting her house in shadows. Two stories with gabled windows and a covered porch, it was painted a dark steel blue with off-white trim and had a maroon door. White daisies flourished along the front. Their glowing white pedals were eerie in the dimming light.

She stepped up the stairs and used her key to unlock the door, glancing around again. When she stepped inside, freshly treated dark wood floors, white trim and neutrally colored walls would normally welcome her. Instead she looked for signs of Jed. Pausing to lock the door, she listened for any sounds. Silence. Nothing had changed since she'd left. Everything was as it had been.

She turned and passed an open stairway on her way to the kitchen, flipping on a light to chase the shadows away. Still, she couldn't shake the apprehension warning her that Jed might reappear. She'd had a bad feeling when he'd started sending her emails. It was as if he was stalking her. She'd shown the emails to Lacy, who'd been concerned and that had made Gemma worry more. He hadn't threatened her in them, only pleaded with her to come home. Creepy. And then he'd shown up in Cold Plains, exactly what she'd feared.

She wondered if Lacy had been the one to tell Samuel about her attack. Lacy had been the first person she'd called. Since she'd moved here, they'd grown close. Gemma met her at the coffee shop and she'd invited her to a seminar. They'd struck up an instant friendship.

After opening the refrigerator, Gemma shut it again, no longer craving iced tea. She was too unsettled, unable to quell the feeling of lurking danger. Her gaze travelled over the soft green cabinets to the colorful window dressings above the darkened window.

She tried to redirect her focus, turning it toward the house she loved so much. All the furniture and appliances were the best money could buy, thanks to a long-building savings account she'd kept secret, and the sizable chunk of money she'd taken from Jed. It wasn't all his money anyway. They'd been married and he'd lost that part of the court proceedings. The judge had given her even more than she'd asked for. Half of everything, and everything was a lot. His parents had left him a fortune before alcoholism killed them in their fifties. She figured Jed owed her anyway, after the way he'd abused her and hoarded their money. He was an animal disguised as a successful orthopedic doctor. He probably enjoyed setting broken bones for the pain it caused his patients.

Lifting her hand, she felt the sore skin around her temple where his fist had split it open. Then she glided it down to her swollen nose and mouth where a cut still stung. She still hurt deep inside her torso but those bruises were healing now. Her leg muscles were sore from trying to kick him or fight free of him. Her shoulders. Her whole body was sore from the violent struggle.

When I come back, you better be ready, he'd hissed in that evil voice she'd learned to dread. Full of warped love. *You'll either come back home with me, or I'll kill you, Gemma.*

Just before letting her battered body drop to the floor of this very room, he'd added, *You're my wife.*

She wasn't. Not anymore. He was just crazy. Pure crazy. Didn't he remember the divorce? He'd been furious with the outcome, with how much the judge had given her of *his* money. Let her take it. *Steal it,* as he'd said. Maybe that was enough to make him snap. He'd snapped long before that, but he'd never threatened to kill her before. It didn't matter. She believed him now.

Sighing, she looked around her beautiful kitchen, small but quaint with tiled countertops sparsely adorned with glass canisters and a basket of red apples. The single white-trimmed back door led to a courtyard-like backyard, bursting with wildflowers, and a terraced vegetable garden. She wished he hadn't attacked her here. He'd poisoned her fresh start. Her new life in a safe town. He'd shaken her security and she hated him for that. She hated herself more for allowing it to happen.

Her mother would say, "I told you so," speaking from experience. She hadn't done any better with her own husband. Mom had always dreamed of finding that special someone who'd take care of her. Take care of everything, including her own thinking. Except she'd missed the part where she had to choose the right man. And now it looked as if she'd passed that lack of talent onto her girls. Gemma had most certainly chosen badly. Her sister, Gillian, didn't appear to want to settle down yet. She was too busy sleeping with every man who'd have her. No good choice in any of them, either.

All Gemma had ever wanted was to find her way. Being raised by a mother who'd struggled to support the three of them had set her back. Not because of the lack of money, because her mother was incapable of taking charge of her own life. Gemma had spent too much time growing up without guidance. She'd needed guidance. It hadn't been until she'd arrived in Cold Plains and met Samuel Grayson that she'd realized that. She was handicapped. But not anymore. Now she had the guidance she so desperately needed. With it, she'd find herself and she'd grow in the right direction and succeed. She'd be whole for the first time in her life.

It was exhilarating. Just knowing she had the power to overcome. Having the affirmation. The support. Her soul was starved for it. Living here gave her a glimmer of real happiness and the hope to prosper. No way was she giving that up. Somehow she'd have to deal with Jed. She'd have to face him, on his terms if necessary. With violence. Somehow she'd find the courage. Right now, though, she had her doubts. His timing couldn't be worse. She was still weak. He'd made her that way. And he meant to keep her that way.

A sound at the front door sent her heart into a frantic rhythm. Someone had just tried the knob. Was Jed back already? He hadn't said how long he'd give her. The sun had set now and it was dark in her living room.

Walking softly to the kitchen drawer, Gemma slid it open and lifted a butcher knife. Next, she went to the table where she'd left her purse and began digging for her cell phone and the card Ford had given her. Clutching both, she went to the front window and peeked around the edge of the swooping deep blue drapes to look through the open wood blinds. She couldn't see very far through the darkness and she hadn't yet turned on her exterior lights.

Her heart throbbed, fear tightening her throat and drying her mouth. What should she do? Had she imagined the sound? No. Someone had tried to open the door. Jed. She'd left it open for him before. Maybe he thought he'd get lucky again.

Going to the front door, she flipped the light switch beside it and peered through the peephole. Nothing. Just as she began to relax, breaking glass from the kitchen made her jump and turn. Jed stood on the other side of her back door, his arm reaching inside to unlock the door.

Screaming, she faced the door again and tried to release the lock. The knife and the phone made it difficult. She couldn't put them down. She had to call for help. But how would she do that? She wouldn't have time. With a frantic glance behind her, she saw Jed storming into her kitchen, deep-set, light gray eyes full of evil. He was almost six feet tall and well-muscled without being stocky. A terrifying sight.

The knife fell to the floor as she released the lock. She yanked open the door just as Jed reached her, grabbing her arm and pulling her back. She lost her balance and fell against one of her wingback chairs, dropping the phone. It bounced to a standstill under the antique coffee table.

Jed slammed the front door shut, a crazy man full of hatred. "Are you *packed?*"

Gemma debated trying to go for the phone. The knife was too far away, and too close to Jed's advancing feet.

"I asked you a question!"

She scrambled around the chair and backward toward the table. "Stay away from me!"

He kept coming toward her, long slow strides full of murderous intent.

Reaching for the phone, she grabbed it and pressed 911. Jed kicked her wrist before she could press Send, and the phone sailed across the room.

Crying out in pain, she rolled out of the way of a second blow and stumbled to her feet. The knife.

It was near the door, on the other side of Jed. She'd have to get past him. Shoving the heavy chair in front of her, she leapt around it, grabbing the painting of an old barn surrounded by a field of wildflowers off the wall on her way. As Jed moved to intercept her, she swung the painting. The thick frame hit him. He blocked any damage it might have done with his arm, but it was enough to knock him off balance. She was able to get past him and ran to the door, stooping to pick up the knife and yanking the door open.

Jed grabbed her around the waist. She stabbed his arm with the knife. He growled in agony and released her. She ran through the door and jumped over the steps of her porch to land on the walkway. She ran across her lawn toward her neighbor's house.

"Help!" she screamed. "Help me!"

She kept screaming and screaming, hoping someone would hear her, hoping Jed would leave.

Across the street, an old woman opened the door. Martha. That was her name. She lived there with her granddaughter. Gemma talked to her every once in a while. She and her granddaughter didn't share much of their lives with anyone. They kept to themselves.

Martha moved out of the way as Gemma ran up the stairs of her porch and bolted through the entrance, scurrying to slam the door shut.

"Great goats! Are you all right?" Martha asked breathlessly, shaking with alarm.

"Call the police!"

Chapter 2

This was the second time Dillon Monroe had followed his dad to this old Victorian inn. The Stillwater used to be the home of a Cold Plains settler who had been driven out of town after Samuel Grayson arrived and started making changes. Why was his dad meeting with that freak and a bunch of knuckle-draggers?

Easing out from behind the thick trunk of a tree, Dillon made his way through a bed of immaculate landscaping that during the day was a palate of weed-free color. There was a lot of that in this town. He stepped up to the front doors and entered the foyer where an ornately trimmed registration desk gleamed beneath a crystal chandelier. A man was speaking to a woman standing there beside him and neither looked at Dillon. To his right, double French doors opened to a dimly lit bar. A woman sat there, a glass of water in front of her. She looked familiar. The owner of Cold Plains Coffee. What was she doing here all by herself? Drinking water in a bar. Weird.

"Good evening, sir."

Turning to his left, he saw another pair of French doors that opened to a room full of candlelit tables covered in white linen underneath two more chandeliers. The brown-eyed hostess behind a wooden stand had just acknowledged him. Dressed in an elegant black dress and sparkling earrings with her dark hair smoothed back into an elegant bun, she fitted Samuel's demands for perfection. She was probably about three years older than Dillon, which put her around twenty-one. He was pretty tall and she was almost to his nose in height. Good-looking, and he didn't miss how she checked him out from his black hair and hazel eyes all the way down his lanky form before she asked, "Your name?"

You had to have reservations to come to a joint like this. He searched for Whack Job Hollywood among the late-evening diners. There weren't many. It was going on ten. "I'm here to see Samuel Grayson."

"Is he expecting you?"

"No. Is he here yet?"

After a few uncertain blinks, her gaze flitted into the foyer. Dillon turned and saw a narrow, open doorway leading down into the basement.

He faced the girl again. "Look, I don't want to cause you any trouble. I just need to speak with him for a minute." He didn't, actually. He was here to find out why his dad was here.

The hostess didn't respond, but glanced around as though checking to see if anyone had heard.

"Pretend I was never here." Smiling at her, he walked out of the dining area. A wider stairway opposite the basement passage led to the upper-level rooms. The man and woman behind the fancy registration counter were still busy talking. The woman in the bar didn't seem to see him.

Dillon reached the threshold of the stairs. Descending them, he entered what appeared to have once been the servants' kitchen and now functioned as the hotel staff's food-prep area for what had to be a small conference center. Heavy wooden double doors probably led to a meeting room. The doors were closed.

Moving closer, he heard muffled voices filtered through from the other side. He put his hand on the door handle and began to push.

"You there!"

Dillon jumped around to see a big burly man approaching him from the stairway. Tall and slick in a suit and tie, he looked as rich as all the other knuckle-draggers Dillon had seen with Grayson. Was his dad trying to become one of them?

"Are you lost?" he asked.

"I was looking for someone." Dillon brushed past the man and climbed the stairs. Back in the foyer, he saw the woman who'd been in the bar standing there, and beyond her, the elaborately coiffed hostess watching nervously from behind her stand. He glanced back and saw the burly man enter the foyer. Time to go.

Outside, artificial light illuminated his way. Past the circular drive, he stepped onto the lawn and looked back to check how safe he was. The big man had stopped on the front porch, holding a radio to his mouth. Safe enough. He wasn't going to follow.

Dillon jumped over a cluster of pansies, his feet crunching on mulch as he maneuvered through the wide and curving border. When darkness cloaked him, he stopped. The knuckle-dragger still stood on the front porch. Dillon moved behind the trunk of a pine tree and waited.

Rustling in some nearby shrubbery made him turn. There was someone there. He walked toward the sound and stopped when he saw a girl. She inhaled her alarm, taking a step back. He recognized her. She was new to town. She and her grandmother had just moved here. She had long, thick, dark brown hair and green eyes, but it was her hot body that had always caught his eye.

"What are you doing here?" he asked.

"What are *you* doing here?" she countered.

Had she recognized him? "Why are you hiding in the trees?"

Pursing her lips, she folded her arms and stuck out a trim hip. "Why are you?"

He chuckled and held out his hand. "I'm Dillon Monroe."

After a brief hesitation, she shook his hand. "Hallie Taylor."

"I know who you are. We go to the same school. Did you come here for dinner?" He knew she hadn't but he played ignorant.

She frowned while she studied him. "You go to Cold Plains High?"

He nodded. She didn't recognize him. "I'm a senior." Or he would be in the fall.

"I'm going to be a junior."

"I know."

"You do?"

"Yeah. I noticed you at school last year. You're new to town, right?"

"Yeah."

There didn't seem to be anything else to say, and they were standing in the landscaping like a couple of delinquents.

Finally, he glanced back at the inn. "Samuel Grayson is in there."

She frowned again, this time from a different kind of curiosity. "Is that why you're here? Did you have dinner with him?"

"No. My parents are friends with him. I can't stand the man."

She seemed to ease her tension, but there was an element of distrust that surrounded her. She did seem really quiet at school. She hung out with one girl and didn't seem to have many other friends. Not popular, but she could be. She was pretty enough. She just wasn't all that outgoing. He wondered if the reason she was here had anything to do with that.

Her gaze shifted and he looked toward the inn again. Samuel emerged with his goons, but someone else with him made Dillon take notice. Chief of Police Bo Fargo.

"I knew it!" Hallie said, moving beside him.

Dillon looked over at her. "I thought you came here for dinner."

Her green eyes moved up to meet his confrontation. "I never said I came here for dinner."

He grinned because she'd fallen right into his trap. If she hadn't come for dinner, why was she here, hiding in the trees?

"I better get going." She started walking toward the road on the other side of the trees that encompassed the inn.

"Hey, I don't care why you were here. I came to spy on Grayson and I'm pretty sure you came to do the same."

She didn't stop or acknowledge him.

He could understand her fear. Her reason for being here had to stay secret. If the wrong person found out, she might catch Grayson's attention.

They reached a bicycle lying on the ground and she picked it up.

Dillon touched her arm to stop her. "My truck is right up the street. I can drive you home."

"I can ride my bike."

Just then a silver BMW drove by with Grayson in the back. He saw them. The BMW passed without stopping and Dillon let his held breath out. That was close.

"Come on, I'll drive you home."

She didn't argue as he took the bike from her and pushed it to his twenty-year-old blue-and-white Chevy truck. While he put it into the back, she looked up the street, chewing her bottom lip.

He opened the passenger door for her and she got inside. Walking around, he sat behind the wheel and started the engine. Hallie told him where she lived but fell into deep thought after he began driving.

"My dad hangs out with Samuel all the time," Dillon put out there. It'd be great if she started talking. Maybe they could team up.

Her gaze moved for a tentative glance but she said nothing.

"That's why I started watching him," he continued as though he hadn't noticed. "I followed him to the inn tonight. I think Samuel did something to change him. Not that my dad was all that great before. He's always treated my mom like dirt. She hates going anywhere with him anymore, but he keeps making her. He likes going to the community center all the time. There's something weird going on there."

Hallie's head turned a small degree, enough for her eyes to once again glance his way.

"My mom's been drinking a lot. I'm starting to get really worried about her."

"Is that why you're following your dad?"

Finally. He'd gotten her to talk. "Yeah. She needs someone to watch over her. My dad's not going to. He's going to drag her into a garbage can."

"That's really sweet. That you're watching over her."

Sweet? He'd kick his dad's behind if he ever hurt his mom again. "I saw a tattoo of *D* on his hip."

"Really?"

"I don't know if my mom has one, but I bet she does. He probably forced her to do it with him." That made him so mad.

"Even if she didn't want to?"

"She drinks way too much. It's like she tries to blot out the fact that he's turning into a whack job and taking her with him. Compliments of Grayson." He didn't even try to hide his disgust. He used to be close to his dad. Now his dad barely noticed when he came and went.

"What are you going to do?" Hallie asked.

Without even telling him, she'd revealed their common interest. They both despised Samuel Grayson.

"Keep following my dad. Maybe I'll catch him or Grayson doing something wrong."

"Are you blind? Bo Fargo was there." Her emotion gave away the reason she'd gone to the inn. Bo Fargo.

He didn't ask her why. She probably wouldn't tell him anyway. "He's one man in a whole police department."

"The Chief of Police."

"Not everyone supports Samuel Grayson."

"Yeah, but who would that be?"

"Ford McCall wasn't at the inn tonight. He doesn't meet Grayson anywhere."

After a moment, she asked, "You think he isn't one of them?"

"He never goes to any of those seminars, and I never see him anywhere Grayson is unless the whole town is there."

They reached the street where she lived. As he drove around the corner, flashing lights elicited a startled gasp from Hallie.

"My grandmother!"

After frantically running to every window and door to make sure they were all locked, Gemma didn't think she'd ever been happier to see firemen and police officers. The five minutes it had taken for them to get here seemed like hours, each second spent frightened out of her mind that Jed would find a way inside Martha's house. The firemen had already checked her out and the police had arrived to ask questions. She and Martha had just finished answering them. Gemma looked for Ford again—she'd done that several times. Where was he?

Gemma joined Martha on the sofa. The woman's gravity-ravaged face and stunning light blue eyes were drawn with strain. She'd given the poor old woman quite a scare.

"I think you saved my life tonight, Martha."

Martha's smile eased the lines of tension. "I haven't had this much excitement since my son went missing. My old ticker can't take much more of that." She patted her chest above her large and sagging breasts.

What she'd said about her son caught Gemma's attention in a hurry. "Your son is missing?"

"Mmm-hmm. Since a few months ago."

"Do you know what happened to him?"

With that, the old woman grew uncertain. "The police say they're looking for him."

It didn't sound as though she believed that.

"They think he left of his own free will," she added.

"But you don't think so?"

What Gemma had thought was uncertainty became something else entirely. Distrust. Martha eyed Gemma with anxious hesitation.

Her discussion with Ford gave her a moment of uncertainty herself. Was there something going on in this town? Something that made Martha suspicious of her neighbors?

Someone burst through the door. Gemma looked up, expecting Ford. When she saw Martha's granddaughter charging into the room, followed by a slightly older boy, she restrained her disappointment. There were plenty of policemen here. She didn't need Ford.

"Grandma!" the girl yelled.

The boy entered the house and stopped just inside.

Using the armrest for support, Martha stood up from the sofa and the girl threw herself against her for a hug. "Oh, my God. Are you okay?"

"Great goats, Hallie, I'm fine. It was our neighbor who

needed help." She leaned back. "Gemma was attacked by her ex-husband again."

The girl glanced down at Gemma and then began touching her grandmother all over as though having to feel for herself that she was all right. It was so moving. Gemma had never had anything like that growing up. She'd never felt that close to her mother.

"We drove up and there were all those lights." Hallie's eyes misted. "I was so scared."

Martha gave her granddaughter a kiss on her cheek. "Oh, now, you see everything is all right."

"I didn't know, with all the trouble we've been —" She shot a look at Gemma. "I just didn't know."

What had the girl stopped herself from saying? Trouble with what? Martha's son? Hallie had to be his daughter.

"Gemma!"

At the sound of the rich, deep voice so full of concern, Gemma looked up to see Ford striding toward her, maneuvering through firemen and police officers to reach her. The sight of him sent sparks of gladness chasing through her. She couldn't explain why. Why was he different than the other officers? She didn't care.

She stood as he neared.

Instead of taking her into his arms as she half-expected, he took her hands and surveyed her. "Are you all right?"

"Yes."

He surveyed her all over again. "Are you sure?"

"I got away before he hurt me." Again.

"Or killed you," he shocked her by saying, reminding her that Jed had promised to take her home…or kill her if she refused. She shuddered.

Ford rubbed her arms. "I should have been there."

He was concerned. Really concerned. More than a police officer should be. Absurdly, this was exactly what she craved. For him to be here, making her feel safe…and more.

Seeming aware of the intimacy at the same moment, he regained his composure. "What happened?"

She reiterated what she'd already told the other officers. "He got away." And that was what bothered her most. When she'd been racing from window to window inside Martha's house, the night had cloaked him. Where was he? When would he show up next? Where would she be? Was he waiting outside? She'd have to watch over her shoulder constantly. And locking her house wouldn't be enough. What was she going to do?

She looked through the darkened window. In daytime she could see her house from here. Now she only saw her porch light. She didn't want to go home. What if he was out there now? Watching the police. Waiting...

"Don't worry, Gemma," Ford said, bringing her gaze up to his gorgeous blue eyes. "I'll find him."

Movement at the front door made her turn with Ford. Bo Fargo entered. Big and tall, walking with an air of steamrolling intensity. He was older, in his fifties, with thinning brown hair. As he drew nearer, his bleary blue eyes drilled her with what she suspected was annoyance and forced concern.

"I heard what happened." He came to a stop next to Ford and asked Gemma, "Are you all right?"

"Yes." She was getting tired of being asked. "Fine."

"You were lucky to get away from him." No mincing of words there. He definitely was a man who demanded respect. But there was something darker there, too.

Averting her gaze, she spotted Hallie handing her grandmother a cup of hot tea. Then she noticed the firemen had gone, and the other officers were beginning to do the same. It left her empty and full of dread. Soon she'd have to face her house alone. The glass in her back door was broken.

"You can stay here for the night."

Gemma turned to see Hallie.

"Right, Grandma?" Hallie asked Martha.

"Of course, dear." Martha looked at Gemma. "We have plenty of room."

"Thank you." The two had no idea what that meant to her. Or maybe they did. But then the way Hallie watched Bo caught her suspicion. She all but glared at the man. The boy she'd entered the house with moved to her side, watching along with her. What was that all about?

"This is the second time Jed Johnson has gotten away, Ford," Bo said. "I thought you were going to assign a patrol to Gemma's house."

Ford's reaction was full of resentment. "I did."

There hadn't been enough time.

"Well, apparently it isn't enough."

"According to whom?"

Gemma did a double take at Ford's retort. Clearly he wasn't afraid of his boss.

The Chief of Police didn't appear offended; challenged, maybe, but not offended or angry. He knew he was in charge. Or thought he was. "We can't have this kind of crime happening here in Cold Plains. It ruins our stellar reputation. Our peace-loving culture. Something like this threatens the morale." He turned to Gemma. "Isn't that right?"

He was asking her? "W-well…I suppose so." She didn't like feeling afraid to go home. Her house was her sanctuary. *Was* her sanctuary. That had been stolen from her. By that worthless wife-beater of an ex-husband she so stupidly married in the first place!

Ooh…she was going to find something really frivolous to blow a sizable chunk of his money on.

Noticing Ford's brooding presence, she wondered what made him dislike Bo.

"A patrol obviously isn't enough," Bo reiterated. "Samuel suggested that it might be a good idea if you stayed with Ms. Johnson until our perpetrator is captured. I happen to agree."

Gemma covered her surprise and saw Ford doing the same. "Samuel wants Ford to stay with me?" To protect her?

Bo smiled, cunning and sureness abounding. Indomitable cunning. "Yes, he does, Ms. Johnson. He was not at all happy to hear that you were attacked again. He cares a great deal about your well-being. He cares even more about the well-being of this town. He would care about any woman who's been brutalized. He wants you to feel safe, and I intend to make sure that you do."

While that sentiment eased a lot of her anxiety in a giant rush, she also hesitated. Samuel seemed to be going overboard for her. Or was Bo accurate when he said he cared about any woman who'd been brutalized? Yes. Samuel was out for the good of the town as a whole.

"Of course, it's ultimately up to you, but I do agree with Samuel that it's in your best interest to have an officer at your house when you're there. You shouldn't be alone until we capture Jed."

"I…" She looked at Ford, whose hard eyes met hers.

"If not Ford, then someone else," Bo looked at Ford expectantly.

"I'll do it," Ford snapped, and then softly to her, "But only if you agree."

Torn, Gemma looked from Ford to Bo and then through the front window. Though her house was still well-lit, it may as well be in Amityville.

Slowly, she met Ford's eyes again. "I would hate to impose on your time…"

"It would be no trouble." Ford's voice was calm and every bit as sure as Bo had been. "I'd rather not risk another attack, either."

She smiled up at him and he looked at her mouth.

"Then it's settled," Bo interrupted. "You'll stay with Gemma until Jed is caught."

"Only if you're sure," Ford said, never moving his gaze from her.

"I have a guest room on the first level. You'll be very comfortable."

"Don't worry about accommodating me, Ms. Johnson. I'll just be doing my job."

Protecting her. Making her feel safe. "Gemma."

"Gemma," he said in his deep voice.

A flutter of excitement warned her to be careful. So did the softening of his blue eyes. The blink that followed cleared it too soon and she felt him withdraw into the role of protector.

"You'll be a lot more comfortable at Gemma's house than that apartment you rent," Bo said. "She's fixed it up into a model of what we like to see here in town."

"It did need a little work when I moved here."

"It's a beautiful place. Cold Plains wouldn't be what it is without good people like you. Rest assured, we'll keep Jed away from you from here on out."

A surge of warm gratitude filled her even while she wondered why he and Samuel were being so kind to her. What was it about this town? Everyone seemed that way. It was almost too good to be true. But too good to be true was her medicine right now.

"I can't tell you what that means to me," she said. "I'm so happy to have found a place to live like this. It's…it's just… what home should be."

Beside her, Ford eyed her askance and then turned his silent watchfulness back to Bo. The negative undercurrents couldn't be missed, leaving Gemma wondering where they came from.

Late afternoon the next day, Gemma watched Ford close the front door after the handyman had finished replacing the window in her back patio door. Before she'd even thought to fix the window, Ford had arranged everything. Now he turned and looked at her. She'd been watching him all day, and he'd caught her many of those times. Starting with breakfast, through his many patrols of her house and yard. All afternoon while he oversaw the handyman and took calls for work. She'd tried to occupy herself with chores. Laundry. The kitchen. Reading. Always he was near, and she was drawn to him.

Staring at him from across the living room grew awkward. She turned away and headed for her back patio, loving her new window and the way it erased Jed's presence. Outside, birds chirped and the sun lit up a clear blue sky. No wind rustled the leaves of her plum tree. Bees visited her wildflower garden. She moved over to the new fountain she'd purchased after the handyman left. It was big, elaborate and expensive, and water trickled over three tiers of beautifully carved stone. She could almost enjoy the pleasure of a simple, warm summer day.

She sat down on her one-of-a-kind, intricately and colorfully tiled patio table and put her feet up on the adjacent chair. Toying with the bracelet on her wrist, she looked down at the dangling sapphires and diamonds. Jed had bought the expensive piece for her. He'd even engraved her name in it. *With love.* She didn't wear it because of that. She wore it for the constant reminder of what marrying a monster had done to her, a reminder of a mistake never to make again. She hadn't kept anything else he'd given her, not that there was much. Falling for Ford as fast as she was couldn't be a step in the right direction. She had to be careful. Take her time. Be decisive. Ford might seem like a good and honest man, a cop, but she needed time to heal from being with someone totally opposite. She couldn't afford to be impulsive with men anymore.

A sound made her look over her shoulder toward the door.

Ford leaned against the doorjamb, eyes partially squinted against the sun in a western sky. He had his hands in the front pockets of his faded jeans and his ankles were crossed. The soft denim fitted him well, resting comfortably at his waist just beneath a flat stomach. And had any man looked sexier in an impeccably pressed, white long-sleeved shirt? The badge clipped over the left side of his muscular chest had to help with that.

Realizing she was really checking him out, she was about to turn away when she noticed him doing the same with her. Their eyes met. She averted hers first, too in danger of giving in to impulse.

"Fountain looks good."

"Thanks."

"Punishing your ex?"

She smiled, hearing his affectionate tone. "Yes."

He chuckled. "Fourth of July is the day after tomorrow."

Was all this small talk masking their brewing attraction? "Yeah. Town's got a big celebration planned." Elaborate. The streets would be lined with flowers and vendors selling food and souvenirs. A band was hired and a huge fireworks display would go off over the park. She'd heard about it all week. It would be the grandest fireworks display in the entire state of Wyoming.

Standing, she moved to the edge of the patio.

"I need you to stay close to me."

She faced him, taking another sneak peek at him in those jeans. "Okay." She'd have done that anyway.

Catching his gaze moving from her chest to her face, she felt as though the fireworks were starting early right here on her back patio. She checked for a wedding ring and didn't see one. Why would a man who looked as good as him not be taken by now? Surely he had to at least have a girlfriend.

"How old are you?" she asked. He didn't look much older than her.

A slight smile toyed with his mouth and then vanished as though he'd curtailed the enjoyment of her question and the possibility that she was interested in more than his protection. "Twenty-eight."

Only three years older than her.

"Your girlfriend must not like you having to stay here," she said, hoping she wasn't being too obvious, a roundabout way of finding out if he was single. And why was she doing that anyway?

He pushed off the door frame and stepped onto the patio, walking in that macho way of his to the edge of the artfully placed stone. "I don't have a girlfriend."

"Does your family live here?"

"I don't have a family."

The flat sound of his tone alerted her curiosity. "None?" Surely he had some kind of family.

He was standing so close to her she could smell his cologne. Nice. Subtle. Deep and just enough spice. But his short answers had her wondering. "What about your parents?"

Looking out into the yard, he didn't respond. Whatever had happened to his parents was painful for him to talk about.

"Don't you have anyone close?" How sad if he didn't.

He turned back to her with much less angst. "Anna. She's my...mother."

Gemma didn't know what to say. Anna was a mother figure to him and he'd obviously lost his real parents somehow.

"She won't be able to stay away," he said with a fond grin, surprising her. He didn't have any trouble talking about Anna. "Knowing I'm shacked up with a woman."

She smiled. "You're working. Bo Fargo told you to stay with me."

"That won't matter. She'll take one look at you and..." He didn't finish.

"And what?" She had to bite back the direct questions popping up in her mind. What had happened to his parents? How had he come to be close to this woman named Anna?

His gaze fell all over her body. "Never mind."

"Too late, Deputy McCall," she coaxed. "What will she think?"

He grunted his amusement. "That there's something going on between us."

"She'd like that?" So would Gemma…

"She's been hounding me lately to settle down again."

Again? "You were married before?"

The tension reappeared beyond the iron wall that shielded his eyes. "What do you want to do for dinner?"

Wow. That was definitely another touchy subject. He didn't like talking about his family or his past relationships. Except for Anna. How odd.

Sensing she'd get no more information out of him, she remembered she was supposed to meet Lacy. "Oh." She checked the time. "I almost forgot. I have to stop by Cold Plains Coffee to pick up Lacy."

"You have plans tonight?" The annoyance in his tone was unmistakable.

What didn't he like? The fact that she had to go out and he'd have to go with her or that it was Lacy she was going to see? "We're going to a seminar."

"You just went to a seminar."

Clearly, he didn't approve of them. "When I called to tell her I couldn't stop by today, she asked if I'd go with her tonight."

After a lengthy pause, he said, "Be careful who you befriend at those."

His warning made her search his eyes to see if he was serious. He was. "Do you mean Lacy?" She laughed a little. Lacy was the friendliest person she'd ever met.

"Haven't you noticed anything odd about the community center?" He turned to face her full-on.

"No. It's modern and beautiful and it serves a wonderful purpose."

"Yeah, yeah. Samuel is a godsend. What would Cold Plains do without him?"

"Why don't you like Samuel?"

"I don't like what he's doing to this town." He sounded disgusted.

She angled her head in question. Why did he think there was something wrong about Cold Plains? "Who wouldn't want to live here?" This was paradise compared to where she'd come from.

He leaned against a post supporting her covered patio. "It wasn't always this way."

"What way? Perfect? Idyllic? Safe?" At least it had been up until Jed showed up.

"This town was full of crime and cowboys before investors came and turned it into a tourist attraction."

He didn't like that? "What's wrong with improving things?" Gemma asked.

"Nothing."

She was pretty sure he thought there was something wrong with it. Why was he a cop here if he hated it so much? "You'd rather have it full of crime?"

"No."

"Then...?"

He stared at her for a long time. "You're new here."

What was that supposed to mean? Old-timers knew something she didn't? She found that so hard to comprehend. Cold Plains was a haven for her.

Straightening from the post, he walked with slow, sure strides to the patio door. "I'll drive you and Lacy to the community center."

Following him into her house, she wondered if the reason he didn't like talking about his family situation had anything to do with his opinion of Cold Plains. She sensed a strong connection between the two. Was he here to right a wrong?

Or did he have some kind of vendetta against certain people? Against Samuel Grayson?

Or Bo Fargo? She'd seen the way he'd looked at the man and it hadn't been friendly. Ford didn't respect the police chief. But why? He wouldn't tell her if she asked. He'd already cut the conversation off.

He led her out the front door and she locked it behind her, watching him scan the neighborhood with trained eyes. She wished he didn't attract her so much. His mysteries kept mounting. And now he'd warned her to be careful who she befriended. Was he one of those she should steer clear of? Instinct told her no. Her heart was drawn to him for some reason. Then again, her heart had been drawn to Jed, too.

She'd be careful all right. She'd be careful not to get too starry-eyed over Ford, police officer or not.

Chapter 3

Gemma entered Cold Plains Coffee as Ford held the door for her. Dismissing the gentlemanly gesture, she looked for Lacy. She couldn't wait to go to tonight's seminar, not for the content, rather, for the break it would give her from the constant temptation to let go of inhibitions.

Rich wood blinds with swooping maroon drapes accented the western decor of Lacy's shop. Buffalo-plaid-patterned chairs and sofas created nooks where patrons could gather. In the center, rugged wooden tables surrounded by cushioned chairs sat beneath exposed beams. The acoustics of the architecture kept the mixture of voices in the half-full space to a muted level.

A middle-aged couple saw them and, after staring a bit, the woman leaned closer to the man and said something that made the man nod and look over again. An elderly woman with a floral sun visor sat at a table and smiled her approval. At first Gemma thought the older woman liked seeing a police officer in the shop, but then she stood in her baby-blue jogging suit and headed toward them, white tennis shoes bright and clean.

"Anna," Ford said flatly.

"Ford," Anna greeted, leaning toward him to plant a kiss on his cheek, Ford lowering his head to accommodate her. "I didn't know you were coming here."

With an affectionate frown, Ford said, "I highly doubt that. What are you doing here, Anna?"

She ignored him and turned to Gemma. "I've heard all about your trouble, dear. And I couldn't be prouder of Ford for helping you."

"I'm very grateful for his protection," Gemma said.

"I told you, I'm working," Ford said.

"That's what you always say. This, however, is different. You call living with a woman working?" Anna gave Gemma a close and deliberate inspection. "A pretty one, too."

"I'm not *living* with her. I'm staying with her for a while. For her *protection.* I'm a police officer."

"And a good one, too."

"Why did you come here? And tell me the truth."

Anna smiled and gave the air in front of her body a sweep with her hands. "I went for a jog. You know I always jog in the evening."

Ford chuckled, a deep, affectionate sound. "So, you decided to stop in for coffee? After a *jog?*"

"No harm in that." Her eyes twinkled with delight.

"You never drink coffee at night. Especially when you jog, Anna."

Anna laughed, the aged sound adorable. The love between them was obvious. She could do no wrong in Ford's eyes. The woman had to be in her seventies and had the energy of a woman twenty years younger. Athletic and thin and nowhere near frail, she was an inspiration.

"I came here to see her for myself."

The entire exchange touched Gemma, and also revealed

a side to Ford she didn't think emerged often. The soft light in his eyes, the soft light of love.

"Anna...?" Ford warned in a teasing way.

"Do you think I'd pass up a chance to meet your new girl? I knew you wouldn't tell me about her and I couldn't wait."

"She isn't my girl."

"No, but you desperately need one." She patted his muscular bicep.

His affection disappeared behind a lowered brow and intensifying eyes. Even with the one person he loved like a mother, he still kept his boundaries firmly in place. Whatever haunted him, it was significant.

"Why don't you bring her by the house this weekend? I'll make us something special for the Fourth of July. You can grill some ribs. Your favorite. I don't feel like attending the fireworks this year. It's changed so much..."

"Anna..." Ford cautioned again. "I told you, I'm working."

"Oh, all right, then when you're finished *working,* bring her by the house. When will that be? Is August enough lead time?"

Ford sighed. "Anna...?"

Lighthearted laughter answered him before she turned to Gemma. "Good to meet you, dear."

Gemma shook her hand, feeling the strength in it. With that, Anna headed for the door. But over her shoulder she called, "When your work is finished, you bring her to see me."

Ford gave her a salute with two fingers, and muttered to Gemma, "She doesn't understand that when my work is finished, I won't be staying with you anymore."

"No?"

He turned a startled look to her. She was just as startled.

"I heard that," Lacy said as she approached, sparing Gemma further embarrassment.

She couldn't believe what she'd said. Of course, she didn't

want Ford to stay after his work was finished…after Jed was taken care of. It was just that Anna seemed so sure.

Hooking her arm with Gemma's, Lacy was about to take her toward the door when all three of them saw Anna pass outside the café window. She winked.

"She may have a point," Lacy said.

"What point?" Gemma asked.

"Are you two ready to go?" Ford stopped the banter irritably.

"When I told her you were staying with Gemma her whole face lit up and she went into this long explanation about how she thought fate had finally stepped in to guide you."

"When did you tell her that?" Gemma asked while Ford's mood darkened all over is face and body language.

"This morning when she came in for coffee."

"That sounds like Anna," Ford said, his mood boomeranging in a way that captivated Gemma.

Lacy grinned her entertainment. "I told her about the day the two of you met. Imagine how intrigued she was."

Ford's mood returned to annoyance. "No imagination necessary. Are you two ready to go now?"

Gemma wasn't. "What did you tell her?"

"Exactly what I saw." Her now mischievous grin left no doubt as to her meaning.

She and Ford had noticed each other. "Ford has orders to stay with me. There's nothing more going on than that."

"Orders," Lacy cooed. "Now that's romantic! Anna thinks so, too."

"You're going to be late."

Gemma noticed Ford's more consistently flat demeanor and Gemma, seeing that, asked, "Are you sure you want to drive us?"

"I wouldn't be doing my job if I didn't." He looked right at Lacy.

Lacy breathed a single laugh and, arm still hooked with Gemma's, headed toward the door.

Ford followed them outside, scanning the street for anything suspicious. He opened the passenger-side door for Gemma. Lacy opened the rear door herself, beaming a knowing smile.

"In all seriousness, Ford," Lacy said from the backseat, "It's truly impressive how well Bo Fargo runs that police department. Gemma is a lucky woman to have your protection."

Only Ford's eyes moved to the rearview mirror.

"You must be so relieved, Gemma. I don't know what I'd do if a man came after me like that. It's so rare when we have that sort of thing in this town. But so comforting to know we have policemen like you, Ford."

Again, Ford's eyes shifted to the rearview mirror. The compliment rolled off him as though he didn't believe her. Didn't he think Lacy was being sincere? Wasn't she?

Gemma looked into the backseat. Lacy's eyes shifted from the rearview mirror. Her smile seemed genuine but her gaze held something else. She turned to the window, leaving Gemma wondering what she was thinking as Ford pulled to a stop in front of the community center.

"I'll be waiting for you when you get out," he said.

Jed would be foolish to try and attack her in a crowd.

"Why don't you come in with us?" Lacy gathered up her purse.

"I don't attend these seminars."

"There's something for everyone. You really should try it," Lacy said.

"No thanks." His gaze pinned her in the rearview mirror.

Gemma stepped out of the front seat and waited for Lacy to come around the SUV, watching Ford walk toward the café where he'd questioned her.

"He's always been the quiet, brooding type," Lacy said as she joined Gemma. "Sexy, though."

Gemma headed for the community center entrance. She refused to talk about sexy. There was something that she did need to know, though. "What happened to his parents?"

"His whole family was murdered when he was a teenager."

Gemma sucked in a breath while Lacy opened one of the community center doors. Murdered? His entire family? No wonder he didn't want to talk about it.

"You can read about it in the newspaper archives at the library. Everybody knows about it. I'm surprised you don't by now."

That was because Ford couldn't talk about it. He kept the pain locked inside.

"There's no question about why he became a cop. And it's no wonder the crime rate in Cold Plains is so low. Ford may not talk about losing his family the way he did, but everybody knows that's why he's such a stickler for the law. Everyone likes that about him. Crime doesn't fit here and he keeps it away."

Gemma liked that about him, too. And Cold Plains as a whole. How could she not? She may have inadvertently led crime to this quiet, peaceful town, but Ford would fight it for her.

She walked beside Lacy into the bustling community center. People were everywhere. Leaving or entering the building, emerging from a hallway, moving into an auditorium and socializing near the tonic-water counter. Lacy told her the water came from Cold Plains Creek and had some kind of healing power. Fountain-of-youth type of thing. She'd have to remember to buy another case of it. At twenty-five dollars a bottle, Jed would be furious if he ever knew.

"I could see you winding up with someone like him," Lacy said, waving to a woman holding a bottle of tonic water.

"Ford?" They entered the auditorium where tonight's seminar was being held.

"He's a cop and he's great-looking."

Yes, a little too much of both. "I don't want to see anyone for a while. I'm still so messed up. I need to figure myself out first, you know?"

Lacy smiled and they took a seat. "Well, you're off to a good start by coming here."

Gemma agreed. "This does make me feel better. I may have made bad choices in the past, but that doesn't mean I have to keep making them."

"That's my girl." She patted Gemma's thigh, as if they were old friends. "That's what Samuel noticed about you. You're eager to improve. I think that's why he's so partial to you."

"He's partial to me?" And why did he care if she was eager to improve? "How do you know that?"

"He told me. He admires anyone with that kind of strength and initiative. He wants you to succeed. The more people who succeed in this town, the better it will be."

While Lacy intended to convey Samuel's good intentions, there was an odd note to the way she spoke of him. Hero worship. Over the top. Samuel admired Gemma and wanted her to succeed. Why did he care that much? As a quite popular motivational speaker, she supposed he would have personal interest in anyone who was striving to go from being abused and downtrodden to thriving. Part of his work. Overcoming the mental side effects of her abuse was her goal. She hadn't known Jed would become violent after she married him. Once she'd discovered that dark side, she'd felt stuck with him. Looking back, she realized that was because he'd beaten down her self-esteem so far that he'd controlled her. He'd controlled her with physical violence.

It hadn't been easy to climb out of that hell and find the courage to leave. That had only been the first step. She hadn't truly begun to feel capable of taking charge of her own destiny until she'd met Samuel and attended one of his seminars. He'd given her hope. He'd given her a light to follow. Light that had restored her self-esteem.

That went against everything Ford had insinuated about the people in this town, about Samuel. She didn't get it. Why was he so negative? The seminars empowered her. They redirected her thinking. Whether Ford thought they were useless or not, they were helping her. Healing her.

A few stragglers entered the auditorium and found seats. The seminar would begin soon. But Gemma couldn't stop thinking about Ford.

"What happened to his family?" she asked. "How were they murdered?"

"Burglars broke into their house. His dad woke up and fought one of them but he was shot. By then the rest of the family was awake. His younger brother was shot and his mother was raped before she was killed. Ford hid through it all. That's the only reason he's alive today. Otherwise, he would have been killed along with them."

"Were the burglars ever caught? How many were there?"

"No. There were two. It's been speculated that they were passing through town."

"How old was he when it happened?"

"Fourteen."

Fourteen. He was just a boy. A boy who'd hidden while his family had been tortured and slaughtered. He'd survived and they'd all died. It was a horror she couldn't begin to imagine. He must have issues with guilt. How could he not? Though there had been nothing he could have done to save them, he might blame himself for not trying. It explained his evasiveness, his refusal to talk about his family.

"That poor man."

"Don't feel sorry for him. He's made a life out of avenging them."

That was no way to make a life.

Sitting back against her seat, Gemma could see how Ford would bottle something like that up, and she could also see how it would lead him to consume himself with law enforcement. But to carry that torch the rest of his life? That heavy burden? A debt he felt he owed? Didn't he see what he was giving up? What did he want out of life? It was one thing to want a career in law enforcement, and quite another to do it out of obligation, forsaking his other needs.

"Ford's a good man, Gemma. You couldn't be in more capable hands."

She nodded. "I know."

"And you're going to be the envy of every single woman in town. A handsome cop staying at your house. Protecting you. How romantic!"

"Needing protection because my ex-husband is trying to kill me isn't what I'd call romantic."

"I saw the way you looked at Ford when you met him."

"Good evening, everyone," the boisterous voice of Samuel Grayson boomed through the microphone. His tall, fit frame moved fluidly across the stage. Not a strand of dark hair was out of place, and his suit was of the finest materials.

"You have the power." He pointed to the audience. "Each and every one of you." He strode to one side of the stage, stopped and strode to the middle again, where he faced forward and turned his head to scan the auditorium.

"You have the power to stop your ego from controlling your thoughts and actions." He strode to the other side of the stage now. "Your ego is hungry for gratification," he nearly shouted, walking back to the center. "It will seek out that gratification at any cost. It will throw you in front of a bus. It will lash out at those around you. Give less to receive more."

Gemma leaned closer to Lacy. "He must be talking about my ex-husband."

Lacy snickered behind her hand.

"Don't ask what your ego wants," Samuel continued. "Ask what *you* want, my fellow citizens." He looked from one side of the auditorium to the other. "What do *you* want?"

"I want a boyfriend," Lacy whispered.

I want Ford, Gemma almost replied.

Ford spotted Bo, dressed in a black uniform and wearing his badge, standing next to Grayson's spread of tables underneath a huge white canopy at the center of the park. Similar in height to Grayson but brawny and unapproachable, Bo was bland in contrast to the community leader's popular appeal. Swarms of admirers flocked near him. This was the place to be if you were anyone in Cold Plains. How many of them had a *D* on their hips?

He guided Gemma underneath the canopy. She wore a crinkly white sundress that scooped low in the front, hinting at bare breasts underneath. Her dainty leather sandals revealed painted toenails and she moved that petite, fit body of hers with smooth and feminine strides, no longer hindered by the injuries she'd sustained from her ex. The healing cuts and bruises on her face were letting her beauty shine through. She looked as hot as the ninety-five-degree day. He was still sweating, and not just from the temperature. It hadn't helped that she'd kept looking over at him, checking out his uniform all the way here, as though his being a cop turned her on.

Reaching Bo and Grayson, Ford braced himself for the show he'd have to put on. They both thought he was their man. He'd like to inform them that he was his own man. But there was a reason he hadn't quit by now.

Passing a table of seafood and a fountain of tonic water, Ford stopped at Samuel, who had his arms around two women smiling and leaning against him, practically drooling in worship. Dressed without a wrinkle in tan slacks and a short-sleeved dark blue shirt, he laughed at something Bo said.

"Gemma," Samuel greeted with the full force of his charismatic presence, removing his arms from the women to approach her. She was the sole focus of his attention now.

Ford watched her warm to it, smiling as she leaned into his embrace. How could it be so easy for her to fall for his bull?

Reminded of her abusive ex-husband, he gave her an allowance. Samuel preyed on people in weakened states like hers. He bolstered them with his seminars and then lured them into his demented circle. He hoped it wasn't too late to save her.

Samuel eased back from Gemma. "I trust Ford is treating you well?"

"I'm never out of his sight." She beamed her radiant smile at Ford, making him falter.

"Good. I'd hate to see you suffer through any more hardship. No woman of Cold Plains should have to go through what you have."

Ford imagined himself throwing up all over the man's overpriced shoes. Or better yet, hauling him off in handcuffs.

"I appreciate your consideration."

Hearing the hint of stiffness in her response, Ford looked over at her. Had she noticed something wrong with Samuel's concern? Did she see it for the manipulative tool it was?

"You deserve a fresh start and I want my town to give that to you. Cold Plains gave that to me when I first arrived. And I'm proud to be a part of such a fine place. Proud of its growth and proud of its people. Everyone should feel safe here."

She smiled warmly, sucked right back into his scheming charm. "Music to my ears."

Ford hoped she was smarter than to allow Samuel to control her the way he did others. That's how he worked. He drew them in and then snared them.

"That's why we have our best watching over you," Bo chimed in.

It was like long fingernails raking a clean chalkboard.

"Catching Jed is only part of the problem," Ford pointed

out. "Everyone seems to forget there are five unsolved murders linked to Cold Plains."

"Five?" Gemma queried.

"His Jane Doe is one of them," Bo sneered, and then said more gently to Gemma, "None of them were murdered in Cold Plains."

"Like I said, they're linked."

"How so?" Gemma asked.

"Samuel, you could probably answer that for her," Ford said. He knew he was pushing it, but he felt it was time to let them both know he wasn't their pawn.

"I'm not familiar with those murders," Samuel said. "They have nothing to do with Cold Plains."

"They all lived here."

"And they all left before they were killed," Bo countered.

All five bodies had been found miles away from Cold Plains, but all five had had a *D* tattooed on their hips. Except one. Jane Doe's *D* had been drawn on with a marker. If Samuel hadn't killed them, he knew who had.

"What about Jane Doe?" Ford asked, watching Grayson. He didn't even flinch. In fact, he appeared bored with the topic. Complacent. He thought he was untouchable right now. Some day his luck would run out.

"Have you made any progress with that computer-enhanced photo?" Bo asked, sounding professional. He easily fell into that role, and it had been convincing when Ford had first started to work for him. Now he knew it was only a facade.

"Not yet."

"Give it a rest for a while. There are more important things to concentrate on right now."

Give it a rest. This wasn't the first time Bo had tried to get him to back off with his investigations, particularly Jane Doe's. And that only made Ford want to work harder to solve her murder.

"Yes, and one of them is standing right next to you," Samuel added, all enchantment and misleading goodwill.

"I don't want to get in the way of Ford's job," Gemma demurred. "He must be very busy." She turned to him. "Five murders. Wow. So many."

"You're his job right now," Bo said. "There are other officers working the murders."

"Of course. I should have thought of that."

"Any sign of Jed Johnson, Ford?" Samuel expertly intervened.

"Not yet." Ford hoped it wouldn't be long before he did have some sign. Living with Gemma was going to be a constant provocation. Keeping his hands off her especially. "But I'm sure he'll turn up soon, and when he does, I'll be ready."

Samuel nodded. "I knew you'd be the best man for the job. I can always count on you."

To do what? The predictable? No one knew he had a private agenda. Well, very few did. Hawk Bledsoe knew, the man the FBI had sent to investigate Samuel Grayson's cult.

Bo and Grayson were suspicious of Ford. They knew he wondered if Grayson was involved in the murders, but were confident he wouldn't get any closer. That kind of ballsy arrogance got to him. Any criminal who thought they could get away with murder got to him. Both men underestimated him.

"Shall we?" he said to Gemma. And then to the two men, "Quite a celebration you have going here."

"Enjoy. Help yourselves," Grayson said, stretching his arm to indicate the tables full of food and that hideous fountain of tonic water. People flocked to it, believing it had some kind of magical power to keep them young and healthy. Fools. All of them. He'd like nothing more than to open their eyes to the truth. Save the entire town from Grayson.

"Thank you," Ford said, putting his hand on Gemma's lower back to steer her away.

She walked close to him, making him aware of her all over again, particularly the neckline of her white sundress. She lifted her hand and shaded her eyes. He noticed a bracelet on her wrist. An expensive one. She wore it a lot.

"Is that Martha's granddaughter?" she asked, stopping.

Following her look, he spotted Hallie and Dillon sitting together on a blanket, talking and eating sandwiches from a picnic cooler.

"Sure is. With Dillon Monroe."

"Monroe… I met his parents the other night. Nice couple."

Ford ignored her reference to those damn seminars, noticing how Dillon watched Grayson's canopy with a low brow. He'd sensed similar tension from him after Gemma had been attacked. Hallie said something to him and his gaze shifted to Ford.

Ford lifted his hand in a salute. Dillon gave a nod of acknowledgment and seemed to regard him differently than he had Grayson. Most in town didn't know which side Ford was on. Those closest to him knew he wasn't a Devotee and never would be. Grayson kept secret the ones he privately tattooed, branded as his own. Sometimes Ford could recognize the ones who didn't belong to that delusional club. Had Dillon recognized the same about him?

Maybe he'd pay the boy a visit. Ask him what his story was when it came to Grayson. He may have a good reason to despise the man, with parents who frequented the community center.

Ford took a step toward the row of vendors cooking food on one side of Grayson's canopy, but Gemma smiled and hooked her arm with his.

"We can't pass up this great food."

He could pass up anything related to Grayson, but her enthusiasm was infectious. Why did she do that to him? Her whole face lit up, reaching deep into her eyes. So genuine.

Maybe that was it. When she smiled, she wasn't faking it, and the result was devastating, for him anyway.

At the seafood table, he picked up a paper plate after she did. They had a couple of hours before the fireworks started. Might as well enjoy it. Trays of salmon, crab legs and tuna were mouthwatering. Gemma obviously had the same tastes as him. She loaded her plate with all the offerings, leaving a little room for pasta salad and steak. She grabbed a roll and would have gone to the tonic-water fountain if Ford hadn't steered her clear of it.

"I'll get us something."

Following her with their identical plates of food to a table under the canopy, he put his down and headed for a smaller tent next to Grayson's. It was selling beer. He got one for Gemma and two waters. Even if she didn't drink it, it'd be worth getting a rise out of Grayson.

Placing the bottle of beer in front of her and then the bottles of regular spring water, not Samuel's tonic water, he caught her look of surprise.

"I'm on duty, but you aren't," he said, sitting next to her. Sticking his fork into the pasta salad, he looked over at Grayson and Bo.

Grayson wore a disapproving frown and Bo sent him a narrow-eyed scowl. Ford inwardly cheered.

A big man with a mobster's face and a barrel stomach approached Grayson. He leaned to his ear and said something. Grayson replied and turned to Bo, giving what appeared to be an order. Ford surveyed everyone around them. No one was close enough to hear the conversation. The two women who'd flirted with Grayson earlier were drinking tonic water from tall crystal flutes with four other women of varying ages.

Bo happened to catch Ford watching. He stared a moment but true to his cocky nature, he dismissed his second-in-command as a threat and lifted his glass of tonic water in greeting. Ford returned the gesture. Bo returned his attention to Grayson and the henchman holding a dark brew.

"Have you tried the crab yet?" Gemma asked.

When he looked over at her, she held a claw in her juice-drenched fingers and her lips were moist. Ford had to gear down. The sight almost gave him a physical jolt.

Putting the shell of the claw onto her plate, she licked her fingers, her soft brown eyes half-closed with pleasure.

Damn.

Her finger-licking slowed as she saw him. Then that smile did its number on him as she laughed at herself.

"Try it!" she protested.

Unable to resist her, he picked up a crab leg and pried it apart. Taking off a bite of the rich, sweet meat with his teeth, he had to agree. Samuel was good for something today.

Finishing his crab, he moved onto the salmon, piling it onto a small piece of toasted rye bread with red onion, cream cheese and capers. He'd rather not get into a discussion on the fact that they had the same taste in food.

"When I first came to Cold Plains, one of the first things I did was find a really expensive restaurant. I spent hundreds of dollars on a lobster dinner. Appetizer. The best wine they had. And dessert. It was fabulous."

She had a thing for spending lots of money.

"Have you ever done that?" she asked.

"Not alone."

"I went with Lacy."

Lacy. He didn't like how close she was getting to her. He'd seen her with Grayson and his crowd. She couldn't be trusted.

"Jed hated taking me out to dinner."

"It's only natural that you'd want to do everything he hated."

"Like spend his money."

"It's yours, too."

"It doesn't feel that way. I didn't earn it."

She felt because she hadn't actually worked for it that it wasn't hers. He commended her for having that integrity, but Jed had been her husband.

"You aren't a special case, Gemma. The law typically divides assets. Fifty-fifty."

"You'd better be careful. Pretty soon you're going to start helping me more than the seminars."

"Then maybe I should be more reckless." He'd rather be the one to help her than those seminars.

"Sounds tempting."

Time to slow this fireball down. "I'm on duty." He tapped his badge.

Her gaze fell to it, then lifted, fueling the fireball. If he had known pointing to his badge would do that to her he never would have done it.

He turned away, watching Bo and Grayson again.

"Don't you ever have any fun?"

Why was she asking that? "When I'm off duty."

That didn't seem to appease her. There was something else she wanted to know.

"Lacy told me about your family."

Assaulted by the uprising of grief that always struck him when he was cornered like this, Ford ignored her, hoping she'd get the hint. Too personal.

"Have you always been in law enforcement?"

That he could answer. "I went to college after the Army and then decided to come home."

"What did you study in college?"

"Criminal science."

"And now you're a cop."

He let her state the obvious.

"You devoted your life to your work," she pressed, and now he saw where she was headed.

He'd devoted his life to law enforcement because of the way his family had died. Clamping down on the flare of resentment she stirred by digging, he leaned back against his chair and waited for her to do what everyone else did.

"What would you have done if that hadn't happened?"

"Can we talk about something else?"

Her brown eyes registered his emotion and she averted her gaze to the throng of delusional, Cold Plains culties. "I'm sorry. I shouldn't have pried. It's just…it's just…"

"You know what it's like to be a victim?"

"No, I didn't mean that…I…" She looked down at the half-eaten food on her plate and it was a moment before she lifted her head.

The sight of her contrition, as genuine as her smile, slammed his defenses. Nothing could change the tortuous sense of loss he felt whenever he was forced to talk about his family, but something about Gemma defused that.

"I probably would have stayed in the military," he said.

Her beautiful eyes met his again.

"I'd wanted to be a soldier since I was a kid."

"It's not too late to go back."

"Reenlist?" He shook his head. "It's more important to me to be here. This is where my parents would have spent the rest of their lives. Besides, being a cop isn't so bad."

"What do you like about it?"

He grinned and pointed to his badge. "This."

She traced its outline with her forefinger. "I like that about it, too."

"I didn't realize how much until I met you," he said before thinking.

She blinked softly and the fireball began rolling again.

Putting her hand on the bench between them, she leaned closer. "Me, either."

He looked down at her plump and ready lips. Something intimate and uncontrollable stirred. He moved the fraction of an inch it would take to press his mouth to hers. Then he jerked back as soon as he realized what he'd done. She made the world around them disappear. The sound of people talking, children playing, the country-and-western band, all of it had become white noise. He'd been so engrossed in her. In talking to her. The things she brought out of him. And above all else, simply in being with her. She led him into treacherous territory, a hurricane of dark emotion that made him seek safer waters.

Except with her, he wasn't sure he'd find them. He felt caught between running and facing the unknown with her.

Chapter 4

After enduring another three hours of enticement with Gemma, including a spectacular fireworks display, Ford dreaded going inside her house. Already he'd come up with several fantasies depicting them in a variety of inventive positions—none of them on a bed. He drew his Escalade to a stop in her gravel driveway—no doubt intentionally left that way to add to the old-fashioned charm of her home. She kept a meticulous lawn, and nothing on the exterior showed signs of a lapse in maintenance. Typical Cold Plains residence.

Ford couldn't say Gemma was typical. Not for this town. Something about her broke down his usual precautions. Was it her vulnerability? When she wasn't trying to escape her ex-husband she wasn't all that vulnerable. He also couldn't forget that she'd taken up a friendship with Lacy Matthews and had not one bad word to say about Samuel Grayson. He didn't want to get involved with a woman who'd wind up getting a *D* tattooed on her hip.

He got out of the SUV and would have walked around to

her side if she hadn't alighted from the vehicle on her own. She'd been quiet all the way here. That quick and casual kiss could have progressed into more. He suspected she felt the same as him; the way she avoided eye contact revealed her own discomfort. Good. Maybe they'd manage this temporary living arrangement without a storm neither of them were prepared to weather.

While she fumbled with her keys to unlock the front door, he checked the street and what he could see of the covered porch. Discreetly, he drew his gun. Gemma stepped aside and let him go in first. He entered the living room, where a lamp chased shadows away. Gemma came inside and locked the door behind her, then waited there. Ford made a quick check of every room and closet downstairs then went upstairs to perform the same surveillance.

When all was clear, he headed for the stairway. With any luck he'd tell Gemma good night and retire to her first-floor guest room, alone. But when he turned the corner, he collided with her. She lost her balance with a small, startled sound, flailing her arms. Catching her around the waist, he stepped down two of the stairs to keep them both from falling. Her hands came against his biceps and her soft brown eyes peered up at his, her lips parted with residual surprise.

Their close contact arrowed straight through his armor. Storm be damned. She slid her hands up his arms to his shoulders, enough of an invitation for him. He leaned down to kiss her. She parted her lips, encouraging him more. Lifting her, he turned and put her on the step above him. Now she was more at his level, though still not taller than him.

This was just like one of his fantasies.

Impassioned beyond awareness of anything but her, he kissed her harder, the fervor to have her too much to bear. He cupped her butt. She had such a nice little butt.

Pulling back to catch her breath, Gemma's passion poured from her eyes as she moved her hands over his chest, running one over his badge, down to the flat plane of his stomach and then back up again, until she put her palms on his cheeks. Rising up onto her toes, she kissed him reverently.

Wrapping her in a firmer embrace, he took over the kiss in a mindless attempt to assuage the fire roaring through him. She lowered her hands and he felt her fingers at the waist of his pants, at the belt that held his gear and gun.

He stopped kissing her and lifted the skirt of her sundress. She pulled it over her head. This was happening too fast. The thought came and went when she tossed the dress down onto the stair beside her and her breasts stood out at him. She was everything he'd imagined when he'd first seen her in the dress. With one arm anchoring her, he bent to take a nipple into his mouth. He was bone-hard for her. No way could he stop now.

Raising his head, he saw her face flushed with equal abandon and couldn't wait any longer. Neither could she. She began tugging harder at his belt. Releasing her, he removed his phone and gun. She took them from him and placed them on the floor at the top of the stairs, out of the way. He slid his belt free and dropped it over the railing. Sitting down on one of the stairs, Gemma leaned backward, arching her body. All she had on was the thong that served as a patch of underwear. The sight of her drove him mad with lust.

Leaning over her, he reached for her underwear. She touched his face and he kissed her while he pulled her thong down her soft, smooth legs. Tossing it over the railing, he pushed his pants down to his ankles and knelt between her knees. He ran his hands up her calves, her thighs, over the curve of her hips, and finally to her breasts. He held them as he kissed them and tasted her with his tongue.

Her hands caressed his rear and his back muscles. He lost his breath and rose up to look at her. Rising up more, he feasted his eyes on every inch of her body.

"Damn," he murmured. "You're so beautiful."

Her fingers curled around his erection and guided him to her. He hooked an arm under her waist and probed her, sinking into her wetness. Her panting breaths mirrored his.

He kissed her hard as he thrust back and forth. She put her hands against the edge of the floor at the top of the stairs to keep from bumping her head. The sight of her was so erotic, so sexually stimulating that he lost himself to it, to her and the gripping intensity of her flesh hugging him as he drove deep and withdrew.

A shattering cry erupted from her, then another, louder one. She kept crying out. He slowed and felt her contractions, doing his best to draw out her pleasure. But the sweet, slow friction drove him beyond his threshold. He thrust harder, pounding into her over and over, catapulting himself into an unbearably sensational release.

Reality returned with brutal speed. With his hands on the top step on either side of her, he met her now-uncertain gaze. Cursing himself for losing control like this, he caught his breath before facing what was sure to come. Awkwardness. Questions on what this meant. Where would it lead?

"Are you all right?" he asked.

"Yes."

"This isn't how I would have planned it." He slid out of her and pulled up his pants.

"That's a relief." She reached for her crumpled sundress and stood to slip it on over her head.

Standing two steps down, he was almost at eye-level with her. But she avoided looking at him. His heart still hammered and he noticed her taking more breaths than normal. The aftereffects lingered.

He took her hand and that got her to look at him warily. While he was so out of sorts with what had just happened, he couldn't leave her alone tonight.

"Let's get some sleep," he said, climbing the stairs.

He let go of her hand when he entered her bedroom.

She avoided looking at him again as she found a night-gown and changed in her master bath. He stripped to his underwear and got under the covers. Shyly, she came to the bed and hesitated before climbing in next to him.

"Do you want me to sleep downstairs?" he asked.

"No." She sounded stiff.

He stared at the ceiling, wishing he didn't have to be here. Something casual was fine. Out-of-control, frenzied passion was not. He didn't want to feel that much with any woman. Not after being married once and losing it all. He wasn't ready for anything that threatened to come close to that. For now, he just wanted to live without any attachments.

"You don't have to stay here if you don't want to."

She'd said it because she felt she had to. A pang of guilt swarmed him. She was staring up at the ceiling, but through the shadows he saw that her face was drawn with strain, distress.

Propping his head on his hand, he touched her chin with his fingers. She looked at him.

"It's not you," he said. "I meant it when I said I wouldn't have planned it that way. It just happened. I wasn't expecting it, that's all." He hadn't seen it coming. He hadn't even thought to check for a *D* on her hip.

"I wasn't, either."

"I shouldn't have allowed it to happen." He slid his hand from her chin to the mattress between them. "I'm on duty."

"If you're worried about me, don't be."

He wasn't convinced. "I'll be more careful from now on."

"I will, too. I don't know what came over me."

Lust came to his mind. Blindsiding lust. "You weren't alone."

"I'm the one who took off my dress."

"If you hadn't, I would have."

She laughed a little and he was glad for the levity.

"Why do I keep doing that?"

"What, taking off your dress? You do that a lot?" he teased.

She smiled that megawatt smile of hers and he found himself enjoying her again, relaxing.

"No." When her smile faded, she explained, "I always act on impulse. I don't think. As a result, I end up making mistakes. Big ones."

Knowing she meant her ex-husband, he didn't take offense. If anything, he was relieved she wasn't putting too much importance on this. He felt less cornered. He'd be able to do his job.

If he could keep his hands off her. The way the chemistry between them had wiped his mind clean of rational thought cast some doubt.

"How did you meet Jed?" he asked.

"I worked in a bar. Where else do you meet losers like that? It was an upscale bar, but a bar nonetheless. I was a waitress."

"And he was one of your customers?"

"Yes. He waited for my shift to get over and I went home with him. No thought. He hung around the bar after that. We started seeing more of each other. In hindsight there were things about him that bothered me, but I didn't do anything about it. He wanted me and that was enough."

"Nothing stopped you from marrying him, so you did?"

"Yes." She rolled her head to look at him. "How did you know?"

He shrugged. He knew people. He was a cop.

"Did something like that happen to you?"

And here's when the questions started. He kept his reluctance from showing. "Not really."

"Something similar?"

"It was different." Much different.

With the long silence, Ford suspected she'd surmised

something significant had happened, something that had made him distant with women.

"Have you ever been married?"

He didn't answer. He couldn't. Thinking of Wynona was too painful. The way he'd lost her...

"You don't have to talk about it," she said.

Again, she defused his tension. She wasn't going to corner him. She'd recognized his difficulty and backed off. She couldn't know what that meant to him. Her insight was keen. Her consideration for his feelings was more than that. No other woman he'd been with had trod so lightly on the tragedies of his past. It went a long way to lowering his defenses, which could turn out to be bad if he wasn't careful.

Crawling closer to him, she rested her head on his chest and put her hand on his stomach. Warmth spread as unexpectedly as when he'd had sex with her. Letting his head sink into the fluffy pillow, he curled his arm around her.

"I grew up with my real mother, but she wasn't much of a mother to me," she said quietly.

The sweetness of her offering worked its way deeper into his defenses. He couldn't talk about his past, but she would tell him about hers. No strings. No conditions, only honesty and selfless acceptance of his unwillingness to share the same.

"My dad left before I was born," she went on. "My sister remembers him but I never met him."

Ford began rubbing her arm with slow, gentle strokes. "You and your mother weren't close?"

Gemma grunted with derision. "No. She needed someone to take care of her. Unfortunately, she didn't have anything to offer a man. She couldn't hold a job and she wasn't very smart. She was raised by a bartender and a drug addict. Never made it through high school. My sister thinks she tried to trick our dad into marrying her and taking care of her. He wasn't anything special, either. He worked at a gas station.

Sometimes I thought she blamed me and my sister for driving him away. She always said he didn't want kids. We grew up poor. I barely graduated from high school and started working in restaurants. Never made it far with that, though. You know the rest."

"Jed Johnson is an orthopedic surgeon."

She didn't question how he knew that. "So I'm sure you can imagine my star-glazed eyes when I met him."

"You married him because he was successful?"

"You're a nice man for not saying *rich*."

He chuckled. He sure liked her good-humored wit. "That explains the fountain."

A breathy laugh answered his. "And the cases of tonic water in the shed. And the house and everything in it. I like spending his money. When it's all gone, I'll get a job. I don't want to be like my mother, with nothing to offer. I read a lot. Always have. I try to stay educated, even though I never went to college."

She didn't care about the money. Not in a materialistic way. But most in Cold Plains wouldn't know that. As far as they saw, she blended into the culture. Grayson's culture. She'd come to town with a lot of money, a young, beautiful, healthy woman.

Ford let that be the end of his questions for now. Like her, he wasn't the type to pry. Damn if he didn't really like that about her. Most people found his dark, tragic history too fascinating to leave alone. Despite how painful it still was for him to talk about, they kept digging for more. Not Gemma. More relaxed than ever, he cautioned himself. *Don't get too comfortable with her. And above all else, don't fall in love.*

Gemma tried not to feel disappointed when Ford didn't kiss her goodbye before she left his Escalade and headed for the front doors of Cold Plains Coffee. They were in public. He was on duty.

She'd fallen asleep against him last night, after talking the way they had. Or she had. He hadn't talked much. That didn't matter, though. She sensed his need for her to take it slow where his past was concerned. She'd also sensed how peaceful he'd gotten after he realized she wasn't going to prod him with questions. Maybe sex on the stairs had meant more than it seemed.

Remembering the feel of his uniform and the way he'd looked making love to her with his shirt and badge still on made her tingle everywhere. Her face grew warm thinking about that.

Entering the shop, she glanced back and saw him still watching and she hoped he watched for reasons other than duty. Inside the shop, the plush interior was full of people. Chatter and the smell of coffee filled the air. She brushed some wayward dark brown hair away from her eye and sight of her bare wrist reminded her that she'd lost her dangling bracelet last night. She normally left it in her jewelry case but it wasn't there when she'd looked for it. What had she done with it? After having such unbelievable sex with Ford, she couldn't recall.

"Gemma!" Lacy walked along the counter toward the end where it opened to the rest of the shop. Her vibrancy befitted the owner of a successful business, so did her love of mornings. Lacy had a special kind of magic with people. Her sunny personality would brighten anyone's day. It certainly had for Gemma the first time she'd met the woman.

Coming around the counter, past a line of three women dressed to the nines and chattering busily, Lacy hooked her arm with Gemma's and whisked her toward a booth. On their way, they saw a tall, thick-muscled man dressed in tan slacks and a sharp-looking black shirt swagger into the shop. He flashed straight, healthy teeth when he saw Lacy. He also checked the entire coffee shop like a celebrity expecting a grand welcome. The man was full of himself.

"Alan? I wasn't expecting you." Lacy leaned in for an intimate hug, the man dwarfing her.

"Samuel is having a fundraiser over at the community center this Saturday. Are you free?"

"For you, I'm always free."

Her infatuation and ego-stroking reply made him smile with masculine satisfaction and glance around the coffee shop to see if anyone had heard how special he was.

Gemma would rather not witness this. "If you two want to talk…"

"I only have a minute," Alan said. "I need to get back to work."

"You could have just called to see if I was free this Saturday."

He lifted her hand and kissed the top, his movements lacking grace due to his bulk. "I had to see your pretty face."

"Oh, Alan. You do know how to make my day."

"Then I'll have to be sure and do that more often." He glanced around again. "And let other men know you're mine."

Gemma searched for somewhere to go. Empty booth, restroom…

Lacy giggled as Alan looped an arm around her waist and tried to pull her against him, an entirely inappropriate thing to do in her place of business.

Gemma was too amazed at his display to move.

"Not here, Alan." Lacy eased away from him and looked for anyone who'd noticed.

Plenty had.

Alan stepped back, loving the attention. "Working here, you must see every single man in town."

"As long as they buy my coffee, who am I to complain? I have two three-year-olds to feed."

Alan seemed to brush over her mention of the children and instead seemed more concerned with marking her as his.

Would he prefer she didn't have kids? Three-year-olds could be a lot to take on, twins were even more work.

Gemma wondered if Lacy had picked up on that. She didn't seem to. In fact, she seemed so taken by Alan, this brute-slash-greaser and aristocrat all in one.

Alan pointed at Lacy with both forefingers, nauseating Gemma. "Be good now."

Lacy gave him a coy little wave.

He finally turned to go.

Watching him swagger out of the shop the same way he'd come in, Gemma felt her brow lift. She turned to Lacy, whose face still glowed with delight.

Baffling.

Rehooking her arm with Gemma's, Lacy tugged her toward the booth again.

"How did you meet that guy?" Gemma asked.

"At a seminar." She sat across from Gemma.

Lacy was sure into that community center. Seeing her new friend sparkling with happiness, Gemma dismissed anything sinister in the reason why.

"What does he do?"

"He works for Samuel over at the community center."

"Doing what?"

Lacy hesitated and the sparkle left her happy face. "I don't know. Whatever Samuel wants him to do, I guess."

Vague. Shady. Didn't that bother her?

"Are you sure he's someone you want to be with?"

With that, Lacy shot an incensed look at her. "Absolutely. It's been three years since the girls' father left me. I'm ready now."

Oh, but Gemma knew all about men who left their children and the aftereffects it could have on them. "What happened to him? Why did he leave?" Maybe that was what had driven Lacy to Samuel's haven.

Just as she suspected, Lacy's face fell into dark somberness, giving her away. "You and I have that in common, Gemma. We both chose badly the first time out."

And she was about to choose badly again from what Gemma had just seen. A waitress appeared with two cups of steaming tea and decadent scones. "Thank you," Gemma said, then turned to Lacy. "You have them trained well."

"I asked her to bring this as soon as I saw you come in the shop."

Gemma studied her friend a while, uncomfortable with prying too much but curious nonetheless. And uneasy.

"My story isn't as dramatic as yours," Lacy said without any probing. "Pretty typical, really. I caught him in bed with another woman when I was eight months pregnant."

"That doesn't sound typical to me. Eight months pregnant? He slept with someone else while you were pregnant?" What kind of effect had that had on her? Would she settle for any man who'd have her just to feel wanted?

Nodding, Lacy picked up a scone and took a bite, chewing with a faraway look.

"You loved him." Gemma could see it plain as day. She probably still did. Well, that helped. If she'd known that kind of love, maybe she wouldn't fall for the same ruse twice.

"Stupidly," Lacy answered with repugnance, relieving Gemma more. "I was madly in love with him. And I was thrilled we were having babies together. I had no idea he was cheating on me. None whatsoever. I was supposed to spend the day with my mother, but when I arrived at her house, she wasn't feeling well so we decided not to go shopping. I stayed with her for a little while but went home early. I heard voices upstairs. There he was in our bed with her, eating cheese and crackers. Must have just finished...and then got hungry. The strangest thoughts went through my head. I remembered buying the cheese and crackers from the grocery store. I felt like she stole them from me."

Instead, she'd stolen Lacy's husband. Gemma reached over

and took the hand that was resting beside her cup of tea. "I'm so sorry, Lacy."

"I think I'd rather he'd beaten me."

She pulled her hand back and leaned against the booth. "No, you wouldn't. I suffered more than this from my ex-husband." She touched the skin near the biggest of her cuts and trailed her fingers over the now almost-clear bruises. "Men who beat their wives do more than physical damage. They beat their self-esteem, too. They erase the woman they married." She lowered her hand to the table. "There's nothing wrong with loving a man. It isn't your fault the one you loved had no honor and integrity."

Lacy smiled softly. "I know you're right, Gemma. My head knows. It's my heart that doesn't always listen."

"Make it listen. Is Alan really worth the risk?"

"I think he is. And besides, it's more than that. Even if we don't last, it's time I moved on. The girls are three now. That's long enough to grieve over a man who never deserved me."

Gemma didn't know what it was like to grieve over a man. Jed had made it easy for her to walk away. Run away.

"What about you?" Lacy asked. "I saw the way you looked at Ford when he dropped you off."

Gemma wasn't prepared to talk about this. Had Lacy deliberately changed the subject?

"How are things going over at your place? Getting all cozy?"

Vivid images of them on the stairs heated her face. The feel of Ford's badge as he moved between her legs. Why did that turn her on so much?

Lacy's head cocked and her mouth opened. "Gemma Johnson, you didn't!"

"Didn't what?" Was it that obvious?

"Your face is beet-red right now." Lacy laughed lightly.

"Stop that."

"I'm not doing anything. You stop turning red or the whole town will know you slept with Ford McCall."

Gemma glanced around to make sure no one heard. "Be quiet!"

"Wow. It didn't take you two very long."

That only renewed her flaming cheeks.

Lacy laughed again. "One of those impulsive things, huh? It just happened?"

"Oh, yeah. Not much thought beforehand. We could have driven over a cliff and not been aware of it." That was the unvarnished truth.

"Hopefully not that devastating."

Devastating to her heart.

"Do you regret it?"

"I'm reminded of your word *stupidly* just now."

"That's a yes?"

Her face began to cool. "My ex-husband tried to kill me. My choice in men isn't very noteworthy."

"Ford is nothing like your ex-husband the wife-beater."

She knew that. "I just don't think I'm ready to trust myself to make smart decisions yet." Or Ford. Could she trust him to be the man she needed? Could she trust him at all in love?

"I didn't think of it that way." Lacy took a moment. "Maybe you're right. Maybe you should stay away from Ford for a while. He's got a lot of baggage. He's a good man, and I can see he's very attracted to you, but…"

"But what?"

"Maybe he isn't so good for you right now."

"Why? Because of the way he lost his family?"

"Oh, I'm sure that's affected him plenty. But…Gemma… he also lost his wife a while back. She died. Five years ago."

Gemma felt a chill of dread flood her, so distressing that she all but stopped breathing. "She died?"

"She was only twenty-two. She died during childbirth."

"The baby?"

"Died with her." Sympathy for Gemma and sadness over the lost infant came through her eyes.

Ford had lost his wife and unborn child. After losing his family to murder. A murder he'd survived. She'd expected some kind of heartache in association with a woman, his wife, but she'd never have guessed it was this tragic. A divorce, sure, but death during childbirth? He hadn't lost only his wife, he'd lost a baby as well.

"They would have had a baby boy. It's so sad, isn't it?"

Beyond sad. Gemma's heart broke for him. And then she felt her guard go up. That was too much drama for her to deal with. How could she ever feel secure with a man like that? He might not beat her, but the feelings he harbored for the wife and son he'd lost would be too much for her to go up against. Her battered self-esteem wouldn't be able to compete.

Ford woke up to the sound of his cell phone going off. Groaning, he rolled over and slid it out of its case. Bo Fargo. At 1:00 a.m.

"Yeah."

"We've got a problem."

He swung his legs over the side of Gemma's guest-room bed.

"Meet me over at the Stillwater Inn. We found Jed Johnson. He was shot in his room tonight."

"He's dead?" Ford stood up and reached for his jeans.

"They don't get any deader. Hurry. I don't want to be out here all night."

While his mind ran away with questions, he dressed and went into the living room, glancing up the stairs. At least he wouldn't have to worry about Gemma while he was gone. Jed was dead.

He had enough to worry about with her. Sleeping with her had him in knots. He felt obligated now. What should he do? Keep seeing her? The idea twisted him into greater knots. He wanted her too much. Every time he looked at her he wanted her. Everything about her electrified his male instincts to the point where he wasn't sure he could control it. That put this whole mess into a territory where he wasn't comfortable. He needed a way out. An escape. But he also didn't want to hurt Gemma.

She seemed to be struggling with the same affliction. When he'd picked her up from the coffee shop, she'd been quiet and distant. He'd asked if she was all right and she'd said yes, but there was tension between them now. Was she thinking about what happened on the stairs? Did she regret it? Part of him hoped so. Another warned that she could be upset over the way he was reacting. And damn if that didn't make him want to run even faster.

Finding his keys, he adjusted his gun and made sure he had his cell phone. Heading for the door, he stopped when it opened and Gemma appeared. She froze in the doorway. He glanced back at the stairs. He hadn't even heard her leave. He faced her again. Had she sneaked outside? What was she doing at this time of night?

"What are you doing up?" she asked.

"I could ask you the same question." Jed was dead…

"I couldn't sleep." Her eyes lowered as she closed the front door, guilt or discomfort of some kind radiating in her body language. He'd either caught her doing something she didn't want him to know about or the sex they'd had was still creating tension.

"Where were you?"

"I lost my bracelet. I thought maybe I lost it between the car and the house."

"You were looking for your bracelet…at 1:00 a.m.?"

"I…I couldn't sleep."

What the hell? Where had she gone? "Why not?"

She rubbed her hands over her jeans, a nervous gesture.

She wasn't even in her pjs. He looked closer. She wasn't dirty or disheveled. She was fully dressed…at one in the morning.

"No reason. Just couldn't sleep."

She was lying.

He stared at her.

Now she fidgeted with her hands, crumbling beneath his steady gaze. Signs of the victim in her, insecurity as the result of abuse, or was it guilt?

"Gemma…"

She couldn't meet his eyes.

He debated telling her he'd just gotten a call about Jed. "What's the real reason you're up at this hour?"

Slowly, she met his gaze, timidity and reluctance clear in her eyes. "Lacy told me about your wife."

That was like a firecracker going off in his face. Anger and resentment quickly followed.

"You asked her about my wife?" Here he'd thought she'd so graciously given him space when she'd likely known all along that she could go to Lacy for all her unanswered questions.

"No. I—I didn't."

He wasn't sure if he should believe her.

"Lacy told me. I didn't ask her."

"Why did she tell you?"

Her hands fidgeted again.

"Why?" he demanded.

His sharp tone made her jolt. "I—I don't know. She thought maybe you weren't good for me right now. With all your…all your…the way you lost your wife."

He caught a flash of hurt before she recovered and it faded into her struggle to remain strong against this obstacle and his domineering confrontation.

His temper eased. This was about losing his wife. She felt insecure because of that. He almost reassured her before he stopped himself. How could he reassure her? This didn't change anything. He didn't want to get serious with her. The way they'd been together on the stairs, what it did to him, what it meant, pushed him away. The way she was reacting to Lacy's revelation intensified that instinct. Did she want more than he could give?

Hell. "We can talk more later. Right now I have to get going."

That's when her insecurity changed to curiosity. "Why? Where do you have to go?"

"Bo called." He wasn't sure he should tell her why just yet.

"Something happened?"

He passed her on the way to the door. "I don't know how long I'll be."

Without looking back, he shut the door behind him. Getting into his Escalade, he drove across town to the Stillwater Inn, alternating thoughts of his wife and Gemma plaguing him all the way there. He didn't know what he'd do, but tonight could make the decision for him. If Gemma had killed Jed...

Flashing lights lit up the tree-filled landscaping and the log structure of the inn. Pulling behind Bo's black Escalade, Ford climbed out and approached the throng of law-enforcement officers.

Ford entered the inn and a policeman directed him up the stairs. At the door of a third-floor room, he went inside and spotted Bo. And then the body hanging from a log beam across the ceiling.

"McCall," Bo greeted him. The Chief's eyes always looked as though he had allergies.

"Chief."

"I guess this means you don't have to stay with Gemma anymore."

"How'd he get up there?" Ford asked, ignoring his comment. Leaving Gemma had its complications.

"Someone used a baseball bat on him first, knocking him out and then winching him up."

"What have you got so far?"

"Not much evidence to go on. No prints. Hotel staff found him."

He looked around the room. Nothing was out of place. "No struggle?"

Bo shook his head. "Must not have seen the bat coming."

"When was he killed?"

"Tonight. We're estimating time of death around two hours ago."

Recent. Gemma entering the house as he'd headed for the door nagged him. "Who called it in? Which staff member?"

"One of the desk clerks. Said he saw the room door open. He went to see if he should close the door and found the body."

"He entered the room?"

"That's what he said."

Ford looked back at the door. It wasn't the kind that swung closed. It stayed open. Why enter the room if all he was doing was checking to see if he should close the door? A maid he'd buy, but a desk clerk? What was a desk clerk doing up where the rooms were? He'd keep that question to himself. Bo might be involved somehow.

"We did find this, though." Bo held up a clear plastic bag that contained a bracelet, an expensive one. Sapphires and diamonds dangled from its circumference. He recognized it immediately.

"Gemma's name is engraved in it."

Mind spinning, Ford struggled with the apparent confirmation of his suspicion. Gemma had said she was looking for the bracelet tonight. She'd been outside in the dead of night. Had she sneaked away and driven here to kill her ex-husband? Why? Revenge? To get him before he got her? Or was something else at play here? He glanced up at the man's body hanging from the beam. Could tiny Gemma have hefted that weight up? Winching him might make it possible. He turned to Bo, who watched him with cunning scrutiny.

Chapter 5

The house was silent. It was beginning to get lighter outside the windows. Gemma hadn't even tried to sleep after Ford left. His suspicion over why she'd been up and outside and his anger over Lacy telling him about his wife kept her anxious. And then he hadn't told her where he was going or why. He'd acted as though he didn't trust her. Had something happened regarding Jed? Ford wouldn't have left her alone if he was worried. The fact that he had gave her a big enough clue.

Jed had been found.

But why hadn't Ford told her? He'd left without answering her question. He was so closed off. More so than usual. He didn't talk about his tragedies but he should have been able to tell her if he'd found Jed or not, and tell her where he was going.

If Jed was found, there would be no reason for Ford to stay with her anymore. No reason other than their intimacy, but that wouldn't be enough for Ford. It would more likely chase him away. While that stung, she was glad something would put distance between them. She needed him to leave her alone. Her reality hadn't changed. She wasn't ready to dive headfirst into another relationship. Jed being found only solved one problem for her. He wouldn't be able to attack her again. Her other problem would take longer. Forgetting him and all he'd done, getting back on her feet again, would take time. And she had to do that on her own. No matter how much she wanted Ford. She'd slept with him without getting to know him first. Their passion had swept them away. Well, that passion had to be controlled from now on. Stopped.

Hearing a vehicle pull into her driveway, Gemma sprang up from the living-room chair and peered through the blinds. Ford was back.

She wrung her hands as she waited for him to come inside. When he did, he stood there looking at her.

"What happened?" she asked.

"Why are you still up?"

"I couldn't sleep." Again. "I didn't know where you went."

He didn't say anything, only studied her as though trying to decide what to say or how to say it.

After a slow blink, he said, "Come and sit down."

Alarm chased through her. What had happened? Something, that was for sure.

"You're scaring me." She followed him into the kitchen and sat at her table while he leaned one hand on it and met her eyes.

"Your ex-husband has been murdered, Gemma."

She sucked in a sharp breath and covered her mouth. After the shock of that eased, she realized she wasn't grief-stricken. Shocked that he was dead, yes. She hadn't expected that. Arrested, yes, not dead. And now she was partly relieved and partly sad. He wouldn't be able to hurt her ever again, but he'd lost his life.

"There wasn't much evidence at the scene," Ford said.

"You don't know who killed him?"

"Not yet."

Who would want to kill Jed? No one knew him here in Cold Plains. "Where was he found? How...?"

"In his room at the Stillwater. He was knocked unconscious and then hanged."

Who would do such a thing? "Did someone follow him here? Maybe he crossed someone back where we lived."

"Do you know of anyone who might have a reason to do that?"

She thought hard, searching through their friends, his professional associates. "No. But then, I didn't really know him that well when I married him, did I? If I had, I wouldn't have married him at all. He could have made enemies. He was a monster."

His observant eyes took in her face. "You feel strongly about that."

She scoffed, her head jerking backward in disbelief. "Well, yeah. Who wouldn't? He threatened to kill me."

"Yes, he did. And he beat you while you were married and attacked you when you left him."

Something about the way Ford was questioning her began to have an interrogative feel to it. She didn't back down. "Monster."

"He was angry that you took half his money. He probably never would have left you alone. He would have kept coming after you."

Now her brow lowered. Was he actually *suspicious* of her? "Ford, why are you grilling me this way?"

He leaned over the table to move closer to her. "Did you kill him?"

She couldn't believe it. "You're serious."

"Did you?"

Planting her hands on his chest, she shoved. "No!"

He straightened, no longer leaning over the table.

She hopped down from the stool and he stepped back to give her room.

"When did you lose your bracelet?" he asked.

She folded her arms. "Why do you want to know about that?"

"When did you lose it?"

Rolling her eyes, she said, "The Fourth. I've been looking for it ever since."

"Including last night?"

"Yes, including last night. I forgot that I put it in my purse on the way home, but I remembered last night. It wasn't there, so I thought maybe it fell out." She was starting to get mad. "Why are you so fixated on my bracelet?"

His demeanor softened. "I remember you putting it there."

The bracelet must have something to do with Jed's murder. "Jed bought it for me when we first met. It's expensive and beautiful. I wear it as a very painful reminder not to make any more mistakes with *men*." She drilled him with a pointed look.

"It was found at the crime scene."

All the blood drained from her face. She breathed to compensate for another jolt of shock that rocked her. "What?"

"Bo showed it to me."

"I didn't kill Jed." Was someone framing her?

"I believe you."

"W-what?" He did? Why had he put her through all his questions? He'd doubted her until he remembered she'd put it into her purse.

"You couldn't have hanged Jed. You're too small. Someone stole the bracelet. Someone who wants to make this look like you killed your ex-husband."

"You think someone stole it?"

"It's the only explanation."

It was. But the bracelet had been in her purse, downstairs near the front door on the small table there. The intruder had been inside the house while they were in bed. She exchanged an unspoken acknowledgment with Ford. They'd been too engaged with having sex and the chaotic emotions that elicited to hear anything.

Someone had stolen her bracelet...

"Why?" This was getting to be too much. First she lived in fear of Jed attacking and killing her, now she was being framed for his murder. "Why would anyone do that?"

"You live in Cold Plains, sweetheart."

Somehow his sarcasm grounded her. She was beginning to see what he meant about this town. Looking into his eyes, Gemma felt warmth consume her.

"You really believe me?"

"It's the only thing that makes sense."

"But you didn't at first."

"I had to be sure."

And now he was.

"What's going to happen now?" The police would name her their prime suspect.

"I'm going to find out who's doing this."

Her protector again. The warmth swimming around in her expanded.

She stepped closer. "I don't know what I'd do without you." She moved her hands over his chest, feeling the metal of his badge under her palm. He put his hands on her hips, his thumbs on her lower belly. His fire lured her. Leaning against him, she slipped her arms around his neck. Then, closing her eyes to the smolder that had begun in his, she pressed a kiss on his mouth. No thought went into it. A whirlpool of relief, gratitude and fear compelled her. That and a deep-seated need to feel safe. Ford made her feel safe.

His hands slid around her and he kissed her back. It felt so good. She angled her head and met his sparring tongue. So incredible.

His arms held her tight against him. She felt his gun, his

phone, all his cop gear, and melted into hot butter. She lifted her leg and he held it up, sliding his other hand to her rear for a licentious glide.

She let her head fall back in ecstasy.

He swore almost inaudibly, a gruff venting of passion, and kissed her arched neck. She began tearing at his shirt. Buttons flew and tapped onto the hardwood floor. He yanked at his belt. She moved back just long enough to unfasten her jeans and kick them off her legs. She'd already taken off her shoes, thank God.

In the next instant, she found herself on the stool she'd vacated and him between her bare thighs. She held on to his shoulders while he found her moist and ready, kissing her hard as he shoved into her with frenzied strokes. The chair rocked unsteadily.

With his hands on her rear, he lifted her and strode into the living room, turning at the now-infamous stairs. She'd never look at them the same way again.

Gently he rested her butt on the fourth one and moved back long enough to take off his pants, his gaze raking over her. She put her heels wide apart on a step. With a moan of desire, he knelt in the space between and reentered her, sliding easily and deliciously into her wetness. She put her hands up as she had before when he began thrusting, falling into a storm of marvelous pleasure. He held himself up by his hands on each side of her waist, his feet on the floor below. His weight pushed down and up as he drove deep inside her and eased off as he withdrew.

The corner of the step dug into her back. Ford slid his arm underneath her, as if reading her. He arched her back more, intensifying the unbearable friction as he plowed his hard erection into her.

Gemma cried out and Ford answered with a kiss. Then he moved his mouth down her neck to her breasts, slowing his movements to spend time there and keeping her orgasm hovering on a precipice.

But then he put his foot up on a step, lifting her leg and increasing the friction as he thrust into her. He strummed her to sizzling release.

Ford didn't stop. Gemma cried out as her orgasm continued. Wild sensations gripped her and then began to taper off. She loved how he met her eyes as he reached his peak, ramming into her two, three more times, groaning.

Then he slowed and stopped, letting some of his weight down onto her as he caught his breath and settled down with her.

Trembling, ears ringing, she closed her eyes. "I can't believe we did this again."

"Damn it to hell." He moved his leg, allowing her to straighten hers, and pulled out of her.

Standing, he jerked his pants on and looked down at her with mounting angst. Too many losses ravaged him, and this overwhelmed him. This uncontrollable connection they had wasn't working for him.

Fine. It wasn't working for her, either.

"Just go," she said. She didn't need to spend another minute with his regrets. Hers, either.

She pushed herself up off the stairs and went to get her jeans.

"You want me to go?"

Slipping her jeans back on, she looked at him. "Jed is dead. It's not like his ghost is going to come to finish the job."

"Gemma…"

"Don't worry about anything. I'm fine. You're fine. But this simply cannot keep happening." She reached out her arm to point to the stairs.

"I know." He scratched his head and raked his fingers through his blond hair. "I don't get it."

"Me, either." But that was the least of her worries. "My ex was just murdered and everyone is going to think I did it."

"We'll see about that."

His faith in her warmed her up a little. "You can't be here anymore. You'll be investigating Jed's murder." Yes, cling to that. He had to leave. Her self-preservation depended on it. He might be second-guessing now, but as soon as his wits returned, he'd be back to his distant self, compliments of his past.

He nodded. And then they fell into a long, tumultuous stare. She wanted him to stay and could see he wanted the same. But logic had to rule for now.

"I'll get my things."

Gemma nodded much the way he had, trying to hide how much it hurt to see how easy it was for him to agree. When he disappeared down the hall, she hugged her middle and kept repeating to herself that this was the right thing to do. It was the right thing. She just wished she felt that way.

The smell of prophylactic paste and some kind of sterile solution made Dillon move a step back from his six-foot-five, hulking dad. Curtis Monroe's round glasses sat crooked on his face. Hair parted to the side was getting gray, and his light brown pants were creased at the tops of his thighs from sitting all day. His appearance clashed with his size. A middle-aged dentist with a serious self-image complex, Curtis Monroe was stuck in his own confused bubble, believing in Samuel Grayson's seminars and dabbling in something secret.

"When are you going to get a job?" his dad asked, and not so nicely. He'd been after him all summer. "You're going to be a senior. It's time you started taking on some responsibility."

"I've been looking." Only cult members or those friendly to them got jobs in this town. But he couldn't tell his dad that. His dad wouldn't listen.

"Not hard enough. You go out tomorrow and stop by the organic food market."

"Okay." It was easier to agree than argue. He had no intention whatsoever of going to a market run by a bunch of crazy people.

He was about to go up the stairs to his room when his mom staggered into the living room from the kitchen, spilling drops of wine from her overfilled glass.

Uh-oh. Here we go again.

His dad saw her and scowled. "Are you drunk again?"

"What are you gonna do about it?" his mom slurred. "Hit me?"

Taken aback at his mom's show of rebellion, Dillon took his foot off the first step and waited. His mother never talked back to his dad. And had his dad hit her again? He looked for signs of bruises and saw none. He'd been hitting her more and more lately.

Ever since his dad had joined Grayson's cult, things had gotten out of control. More and more Dillon felt that he had to watch over his mom. Her drinking was getting bad. The rumors were spreading, too. He was worried she'd be the next one driven out of Cold Plains. There were no drunks here.

"We were supposed to go to the community center tonight," his dad said.

"Go yourself."

Curtis was speechless for a moment. Dillon moved a little closer, in case his dad started swinging his fists. His dad was big but Dillon was, too. Not as thick, but almost as tall, and though his muscles were leaner, he was more agile.

"You're going with me."

"I'm staying right here with my bottle of wine. It's a lot more entertaining than you are."

"You will not! Now do what I tell you and go gargle with something."

"I'm not your daughter, I'm your wife, so stop ordering me around. I'm staying here, and I'm drinking!"

"You need those seminars more than I do. You're turning into a drunk! You're starting to ruin our reputation."

"Good, then maybe we can get our old lives back," she slurred some more.

His dad started to storm toward her, fists clenched and his big body intimidating. That's what had always made Dillon cower. But not anymore. He stepped in his dad's way and planted his hand on his chest, stopping him.

"You got a problem?" his dad challenged, looking down at Dillon's hand and back up again.

Dillon had reached his limit. No longer could he stand by and watch his dad beat his mom. Once smart, happy, loving and beautiful, now she was a shell of that woman. Unhappy. Dull. Cringing in fear of her husband. They both cringed in fear of him.

No more.

His dad pushed his shoulder, giving him a jerk. "I asked you a question, boy."

Dillon stepped right back up to his dad. "Yeah, I do have a problem. And it's you!" He shoved his dad, sending him a stumbling backward.

Astonished, his dad stared for a few seconds, and then recovered with an angry furrow shadowing his cold brown eyes. "What do you think you're doing?"

"If you want to keep going to those stupid seminars, go alone."

Rage contorted his father's round, pudgy face. "Don't you talk back to me like that!"

"I'll talk to you any way I like."

His dad stepped closer. Dillon didn't back down. The fear he'd always felt for his abusive father was gone now. He didn't move an inch and met his father's angry eyes dead-on.

"It's good for her to go to them. She's drinking too much."

"Maybe she drinks to put up with you."

Once again astonished, Curtis replied, "What's gotten into you?"

"I'm sick of you and I'm sick of watching you let Samuel Grayson treat you like a pawn. You're letting him run your life. He's manipulating you. Can't you see that?"

"Samuel made this town what it is."

"A circus? Yeah, he sure did."

Trigger-quick temper flaring, his dad raised a fist that Dillon caught in one hand. He squeezed hard. He stumbled back again.

"I'm not a little kid anymore," he growled. "I won't let you hit me or my mom."

That caused a flicker of doubt to test the coldness in Curtis's eyes. Coldness won. "You were always a disappointment. I should force you to go with us to those seminars. Maybe ask Samuel to give you a few private lessons. It would do you some good. Look at you. You have no ambition to succeed in life. You don't have a job and your grades are bad."

"I'm still in school and my grades aren't bad. My GPA is three-point-eight. Not that you'd know, as little as you've been paying attention. All you care about is getting your way, and if we don't give it to you, you start hitting."

Flashing rage swarmed Curtis's eyes and puckered his lips. "Don't you talk back to me. I'm your father!"

"You're not my father. Not anymore. I won't call any man who beats my mother a father."

Curtis tried to punch Dillon again. Dillon easily avoided the swing and then shoved his dad hard. He stumbled back again.

Stalking forward, Dillon put his face very close to his dad's. "Leave my mother alone. If she doesn't want to go to those seminars, she doesn't have to."

"Dillon…"

At the sound of his mother's pleading voice, he saw that

she'd put her glass of wine down on the buffet next to the dining-room table.

"It's all right. I'll go with him."

"Mother, you don't have to. This has gone on long enough. It's time it stopped. I can protect you from him." He gestured toward his pathetic excuse for a dad.

"I don't want you two to fight over it." She turned to Curtis. "I'll go brush my teeth and we'll go to tonight's seminar.

"Mother, no." He approached her. As he drew near, he saw pain in her eyes. Pain she tried to drown in wine.

"I don't want you to fight. He's your father, Dillon."

Whether he liked it or not. He turned to glare at his dad, who met the look with triumph.

"I'll wait for you right here, honey," Curtis said.

"Mother," Dillon tried once more. "At least think about it. You don't have to keep doing this. You don't have to stay with him. We can go somewhere else and start over. I can take care of you. I only have one more year of high school left. I can get a part-time job—"

"Dillon—" she stopped him "—don't."

"Mom." How could he reach her? He didn't know how much wine she'd had, but he was pretty sure that was what had her backing down.

She touched his cheek and smiled at him. "I married your father for a reason. He isn't trying to go against you, Dillon."

Yeah, right. "He beats you. It's okay if you leave him."

"She doesn't want to leave me."

Dillon turned and faced his dad, making sure he stood between him and his mom.

"I should make you come with us tonight," his father said, calmer now that he had his wife under control again. "You'd learn what it takes to be worthy of this town. If I didn't know you'd make a fool of us all, I would."

More likely his father was afraid Dillon would make *him*

look like a fool. And he was right. "Does that tattoo on your hip make you worthy?"

His father's mouth hung open with shock.

"Yeah, I know all about that. Does Mom have one?" He looked at her.

When she lowered her head, he knew she did. Anger billowed up and consumed him. He faced his dad, ready to start a fight.

"You made her do it?" he demanded.

"Stay out of that, Dillon. You don't know what you're meddling in."

"Doesn't it matter that she didn't want to?"

"It's just a harmless tattoo, Dillon," his mom said. "It doesn't mean anything."

With that, Curtis shot his wife an incensed look.

Dillon got his dad's attention back by jabbing his finger against his chest. "If you hurt her at all, in any way—" lowering his hand, he moved closer, so he looked right into his dad's eyes "—I'll come after you."

"Dillon," his mother breathed, upset again.

Getting the response he desired from his father, Dillon backed off. No longer was he a boy who Curtis could push around. His son had grown into a man who could fight back.

"It was like someone turned a switch on me." Gemma walked beside Lacy in the parking lot of the community center, cringing over the memory. "One minute he's telling me someone is framing me, and the next I'm throwing myself at him. I'm a female version of Pepé Le Pew. Desperate. Easy." Her grimace came out with an *ugh* sound.

"The pornographic version?"

Gemma shot her a look. "Is there one?"

Lacy laughed. "Not that I'm aware of. You could do better than a skunk if you made one yourself, darling."

"This isn't helping me."

"Well, he isn't staying with you anymore, so you don't have to worry anymore."

Because Jed was murdered. "Yeah, unless I'm thrown in jail for murder."

"Samuel won't let that happen."

Samuel? Didn't she mean Ford? How would Samuel stop her from being arrested? Before she could ask, Lacy led her into the community center. Samuel stood in the huge open space of the entry, greeting everyone with his usual suave sophistication. He was like a breath of fresh air. Dark-haired and handsome, a ready smile and an endless supply of uplifting words. No wonder all the women in town swooned whenever he appeared. Except for her. No, that was Ford's area of expertise. He made her swoon without even trying.

Watching Samuel greet everyone who approached him, she couldn't understand how anyone would think he was a threat. His goal was to help people, not hurt them, at least as far as she could see. Or was it what she *wanted* to see? Was she denying the rest? Like his concern for her. Was it concern or was it manipulation? She preferred concern. And why did she? Because she refused to give up the seminars.

Samuel saw her and Lacy and beamed. "Gemma!"

The crowd parted and he approached and opened his arms. She went into his embrace. He made it so easy.

With his hands still on her shoulders, he leaned back and looked her over with approval. "You look radiant."

It must be all the sex she'd been having. "Thank you."

"Lacy, I have to commend you for introducing her to our group. She makes a fine addition."

A fine addition? Like a piece of an art collection? "I think an angel led me to you." Whether he had ignoble motives or not.

He chuckled with the compliment. "I'm having a pool party next week at the Stillwater, on Saturday afternoon. Why don't you plan to attend?"

Why did it sound as if he wasn't asking? It was more of a demand.

"I'd love to."

He turned to Lacy. "She no longer needs Ford's protection, so why don't you bring her?"

"Of course," Lacy replied.

"Don't you worry about Jed, Gemma. We'll get to the bottom of that."

Gemma was afraid her wariness was obvious. Did Samuel think he had that much influence on the law?

"My party is just what you need. It will be an enlightening affair." He said the last with a playful light to his eyes. "Spa treatments. Pedicures. Massages. Anything you desire to fill yourself with the power of confidence and health. Consider it therapy. A follow-up to today's topic."

Today's topic was overcoming negative relationships. She'd been looking forward to it all week.

"I can't get enough of that."

"Someday you will. Someday you'll graduate beyond this level and grow to the next."

"And what level is that?"

"One step at a time, dear Gemma. One step at a time."

Gemma smiled and shared a glance with Lacy, who didn't smile back. Didn't she like what Samuel suggested? Did she know what his next step was?

"There is something I'd like to discuss with you, and the party will be a perfect time," Samuel said.

"What would you like to discuss?"

"I can help you plan for your future here in Cold Plains, Gemma. I know of an investment opportunity that might interest you."

She hadn't thought about investing the money she'd gotten from her divorce. "I'm already interested."

"A woman like you has to keep her finances in order. With my help, you'll never have to work again."

She wondered what he would gain from helping her. She didn't care if she had to work, but if she invested Jed's money, it would be like laundering it, cleansing it of his poison.

"Thank you for looking out for me, Samuel." He was always doing that. He didn't even know her very well and he always had her best interests in mind. At least, it seemed that way. "I can't wait for your party."

"I look forward to seeing you, then." With that, he returned to his adoring throng. He was a celebrity. Cold Plains had a star and it was Samuel Grayson.

Chapter 6

Ford would have left a half hour ago if he hadn't seen Gemma among the crowd at the Stillwater Inn. Samuel was throwing an elaborate party at his latest haunt. Towering fountains. A crystalline pool. Servants with trays of tonic water. Masseuses. Pedicurists at the feet of the wealthy. Fake laughter completed the orgy. It didn't seem to matter that a man had been murdered in one of the inn's rooms. Unless something about that was significant. Why had Samuel chosen this venue for his event?

From his hiding spot behind a thick island of shrubs and blooming flowers, Ford watched a woman lean back on her lawn chair and arch her back as she poured a bottle of tonic water over her body. Did she think it would make her live forever?

Having watched Gemma talking to Samuel for a good forty-five minutes now, he had to stop himself from charging in there and dragging her out by her shiny dark hair. He hadn't seen her since he left her house a week ago. Thoughts of her had weighed on him. He had to force himself to stay away from Cold Plains Coffee on the off chance he'd run into her. He'd been starved for just the sight of her. To see her here shot him through with disappointment. And something else he was reluctant to name.

The swelling on her nose was gone. The cuts on her face were faint scars and there were no more traces of the bruises. He couldn't have prepared himself for her beauty.

What was Grayson saying to her? Whatever it was, she loved every word. She glowed. She smiled. She laughed. Had a week been long enough for him to get his tentacles into her? Was she yielding to his will?

Seeing her flash another one of her magnificent smiles at the man, Ford clenched his fists. Was she attracted to him? Grayson was handsome and adept at hiding his psychosis behind a magnetizing personality. People fell for him and his ideology. What would Ford do if Gemma became one of them? What would he do if Grayson wanted her to be more than another Devotee?

Kill him. He pictured his hand clasped at Grayson's neck, choking the breath out of him. And then, just as quickly, he got hold of himself. He ran his fingers through his hair, hoping this damn party would end soon, or at least that Gemma would leave.

He endured Grayson handing Gemma a business card and her nodding agreement over whatever he said. He endured him kissing her cheek. And then, at last, the party began to thin. Everyone had already eaten the barbecued lamb and about thirty other dishes, all prepared with health in mind. Health and richness befitting a man with power and money. Befitting a town that demanded both from its citizens. Perfection.

Ford slipped away from the cluster of vegetation and headed for the front of the building, stopping before the doors where he wouldn't miss Gemma. He didn't want to admit why he felt so driven to have it out with her, only knew there was no stopping him. Watching her had worked him up into a lather. Dressed in an ocean-blue bikini and a matching sheer sarong, she was a vision for his hungry eyes. She'd left her hair down and her sunglasses made her look like a movie star. Just like Grayson.

That's what ate him up the most. Just watching her stirred a roaring flame of desire in him, and yet she fitted into this crowd so well. She looked as if she belonged among them— the rich and flawless.

She and Lacy emerged from the inn. He should just turn around and leave. Something kept his feet still. His ire. His passion. Emotion he couldn't control at the moment.

Lacy pointed him out. Gemma's smile faded, though her face still glowed from her afternoon of fun and pampering and Grayson's sinister ministrations. Nails freshly painted, skin bronzed from the sun, she was striking. Her trim, petite body didn't have an ounce of fat on it.

"Ford." Surprise marked her tone.

"Having a nice afternoon?"

She exchanged a glance with Lacy.

"I'll wait for you in my car," Lacy said.

"Okay." Gemma turned back to him. "What are you doing here? Did something happen?" She looked around.

He wouldn't reveal that he'd followed Bo here. "Are you getting personal invitations to Grayson's events now?"

"It was a harmless pool party."

"Yeah. Real harmless. Your ex-husband was murdered here and Grayson had the whole afternoon to work you over."

"Work..." Her eyes flashed with anger. "He wasn't working me over."

"Why'd he give you a business card?"

"You were spying on me?"

"Does he want your money?"

That made her flinch a little. "He talked to me about an investment opportunity."

"One I'm sure he'll benefit from. Open your eyes, Gemma. He's interested in more than your pretty face." He hoped that was all.

"What's the matter with you?"

"I saw the way you were with him. Are you going to let him give you a tattoo now?" He couldn't contain himself, and worse, he didn't understand the degree of his emotion. Why did seeing her enjoying the company of another man bother him so much? The answer taunted him.

It took her a moment to respond, during which she studied him incredulously. "What's wrong?"

"Are you?"

"That's ridiculous. Samuel doesn't tattoo anyone. I've heard all the rumors and I don't believe them. Why do you think Samuel would do that?"

"Who do you think arranged for your bracelet to be planted by Jed's body?"

She scoffed. "That wasn't Samuel."

The way she said his name inflamed him further. An afternoon trapped in Samuel's disingenuous web had already polluted her rationale. "I keep having to remind myself that you're new here, so I'll overlook your ignorance."

"Why are you so mad?"

"Because you're here, having a great time with that… killer."

Her eyes widened. "Don't you think that's pushing it?"

"The rumors are true, Gemma. People do get his tattoos. His Devotees are brainwashed to follow him. And if he decides they aren't perfect or if they disagree with him, they disappear. Sometimes they die."

A long silence passed while she absorbed that. "Why do you care so much?"

Her question stopped him short. "Why do I care that you're enchanted by a psychopath?"

"Samuel isn't a psychopath."

He should have expected her to deny Grayson was anything but a savior. "Stop saying his name."

"You're jealous."

He ignored that. "It means nothing to you that the rumors are all true?"

She hesitated. "You don't know that."

"Yes, I do."

"What proof do you have?"

"Dead bodies keep piling up and Grayson is behind every single one of them. One way or another."

"That's not proof. That's your opinion."

"In this case, my opinion happens to be right. I don't need proof. I've seen enough to know what he's capable of."

She considered him with new insight. "I'll ask you again. Why do you care so much?"

About her. That's what she was asking. He didn't know if she believed him about the murders and she wasn't going to tell him. She wanted to know if he cared. When the answer—*yes*—came into his mind, a trapped feeling quickly followed. He did care. He cared enough to let temptation overrule. Except, he could never forget how it felt to lose someone he loved, and he couldn't risk that again.

"I care about anyone who falls prey to Samuel Grayson," he said at last.

The inquiring look in her eyes clouded with disappointment. "I'm not your problem anymore, Ford. If I decide to see Samuel, I'll see him." She started walking toward Lacy's Mercedes sedan.

Ford caught up to her. "Gemma. I don't want you anywhere near him."

"That's not your call to make."

She was upset because he hadn't told her he cared the way

she hoped. Just when she was about to go around the back of the parallel-parked sedan, he grasped her arm and eased her to a stop.

"Gemma…" So much confusing emotion jumbled up his mind that he couldn't organize it all. "He's dangerous."

"I don't see it that way."

Somehow he had to convince her. "You haven't noticed anything strange? Nothing? No matter how small?"

With that she averted her head. She had noticed something.

"Promise me you won't go near him anymore. No more seminars. No more glamorous parties."

"I like the seminars. They help me."

"I know they do." Under false perceptions. "Can't you find a therapist instead?"

"I don't need therapy."

The seminars were a form of therapy. "Then buy some self-help books. Just don't go near Grayson anymore."

She searched his eyes. "Why are you so jealous?"

"I'm not…" Even as he said it he knew it was a lie. "All right. I am. I would be jealous of any man who makes you laugh the way Grayson made you laugh today. But that has nothing to do with why I don't want you anywhere near him."

A smile reserved only for him dazzled her face. The light reached her eyes and he was captivated.

"Stop doing that," he said.

That only rewarded him with an all-out, megawatt smile. She was killing him.

Putting her hand on his chest and moving closer, she said huskily, "You know what I think?"

He was afraid to ask.

She slid her other hand onto his chest and pressed her body against his. "I think—" her hands ran up over his shoulders and he thought he'd die right then "—you're afraid of what this means."

"What's that?"

Rising up onto her toes, she pressed her warm, soft lips to his. "That."

Unable to resist her, he wrapped his arm around her and held her head as he kissed her the way she'd encouraged him to. When he finished, it took all of his willpower to release her and step back.

"Stay away from Grayson," he said, her sultry expression making it exceedingly difficult for him to turn and walk away.

As though hypnotized, Gemma got into Lacy's car, sitting in the passenger seat, staring through the windshield, still reeling from that kiss. The sun was low in the sky but the clear day was still bright and warm, adding to the array of awe singing inside her.

"That man's got it bad for you," Lacy said.

"Huh" was all she could muster.

"I mean, I knew he liked you, but…whoa. I've never seen a man kiss a girl like that."

"Yeah."

"Hot sex is one thing, but that…that is something different, honey."

That brought her out of her hypnosis. "What?"

"He's madly in love with you."

"No, he isn't!"

"Yes, he is. And you're in love with him."

"I am not." She swatted her hand through the air with the ridiculous idea, while anxiety churned her stomach sour.

"Neither of you knows it yet, that's all." Lacy chuckled. "It's just like the movies."

"You said he had too much baggage."

"That was before I saw him kiss you." Lacy drove away from the inn. "And I'd like to see you happy, Gemma."

She believed that's what Lacy genuinely wanted, but falling in love with Ford wasn't a smart thing to do. Neither was getting pregnant…

Panic stirred her anxiety to a new level. She hadn't gotten her period this month. If she was pregnant, she couldn't depend on Ford to be there for her.

Oh, God, what if she was…?

"It could be worse," Lacy said as she drove. "You could be dealing with Alan."

Gemma didn't miss the subtle confession. "What's going on with him?"

"He's mad that I went to this party without him. He wasn't invited. Samuel made it clear this was invitation-only. And Alan had to work anyway. I don't know why he's so mad."

"Doesn't he work for Samuel?"

"He doesn't report directly to him."

"What does he do?" Gemma hoped to get an answer out of her this time.

Lacy shrugged as though it didn't matter. "Probably something over at the community center."

"You mean you don't know what he does for Samuel?"

"He supports the community center."

Her vagueness made her suspicious. "Why did you go to the party if your boyfriend had such a big problem with it?"

"Are you kidding? Turn down an invitation from Samuel? No way!"

"What would he do if you politely declined? Kill you?" Gemma laughed halfheartedly. She wasn't actually sure the answer would be no.

"No, but he might run me out of town. I wouldn't be able to go to the seminars anymore. I'd be an outcast."

Run her out of town? Apprehension clamped down on her hope that nothing was wrong with Samuel and the sanctuary she'd found in Cold Plains. "For not going to a party? What if you were in the hospital?"

"Having to go to the hospital would be worse. Samuel hates illness of any kind. We have to stay healthy."

That sounded terrible. Did Lacy hear herself? And who encompassed the *we* she'd referenced? "Are you serious? He'd run you out of town if you didn't do what he expected or got sick?"

"I've heard rumors, that's all."

Gemma went still. Lacy was backpedaling now. Surely Ford couldn't be right. He couldn't be. The seminars. What would she do without them? Cold Plains couldn't turn out to be something different than what she'd seen when she'd first arrived. It couldn't. "You believe them?"

"I don't know. I've heard people…" Her voice trailed off.

"I've heard similar rumors, too, Lacy. People have been locked in the basement of the community center, and there've been some murders linked to Cold Plains. Some say Samuel is responsible."

If he decides they aren't perfect or they disagree with him, they disappear. Sometimes they die…

"You've been listening to Ford too much. I mean, Ford is against Samuel, and Samuel cares about you."

Did he? She was beginning to wonder. Maybe what Lacy really meant was Samuel had targeted her. But for what? To be his next Devotee?

Is that why Lacy was so vague when she talked about Alan? Was he a Devotee? Was she? Gemma studied her friend as she tried to grasp the ramifications. It would explain why Lacy kept warning her about Ford, and why the rumors frightened her. They were true.

And yet, Lacy was desperate to hang on to the seminars and what she must see as an elite membership to Samuel's inner circle.

"I just can't see Samuel doing those things." Lacy shook her head. "He's a wonderful, positive influence on this town. On me. We can't believe everything we hear."

A short while ago, Gemma would have agreed. It was so implausible that Samuel could be anything other than what he appeared to be, a good and honest man. She could see the inconsistencies now. Lacy was afraid of the rumors, but only because of what she'd lose if they were true and she fell victim to them. Gemma felt a rift begin to form. If Lacy was a Devotee, how could they remain friends?

Looking over at her as she pulled into the driveway and stopped, Gemma wanted to ask her more questions, reassure herself that her fears were unfounded, convince her not to follow the wrong path.

"Would you like to come in for a while?"

"I have to get home," Lacy dispelled that possibility. "The sitter is waiting for me and I can't wait to show my girls what I bought before I came to pick you up for the party. Take a look." She reached behind the passenger seat and came back with a shopping bag. "I felt like you today, spending money frivolously. But I couldn't pass these up."

Gemma opened the bag to see two pairs of tiny bright-red shoes with enough sparkles to delight any three-year-old. "They're going to love them."

In light of Lacy's joy, Gemma lost her ambition to talk more about Samuel.

"Pick me up tomorrow night and I'll tell you all about it," Lacy said.

"Sure." The words she felt drawn to say got tangled in a yarn ball in her throat.

Deciding to table her questions for now, she got out of the car and waved. Lacy waved back and drove the Mercedes out of the driveway.

Gemma went into her house, putting her beach bag down next to the door and heading for the stairs to go up and take a shower. It was so nice to be home and not be afraid that Jed was going to pop out of nowhere and attack her.

The doorbell stopped her, giving her a jolt. She wasn't

expecting anyone. Reminding herself that she didn't have to be afraid anymore, she walked to the door. Maybe Lacy had come back.

She looked through the peephole. Definitely not Lacy. She didn't recognize the trim, average-height man standing there. He held a laptop case and was dressed in jeans and a light blue short-sleeved shirt. His hair was cut short and neat. Nothing about him seemed menacing.

She opened the door a crack, ready to slam it shut if she had to.

"Ms. Johnson?" he asked.

He knew her name.

"I'm David Retting. I'm a desk clerk over at the Stillwater Inn where your ex-husband stayed. May I talk to you?" He glanced around him as though fearing he'd be seen.

"How do you know my name?"

"I read about your ex-husband in the paper, and I heard your bracelet was found at the scene and that you were being questioned in connection with his murder. I know for a fact you didn't do it."

"How?" Alarm and hope collided in her.

She looked down at the laptop case and let him in.

Going into the kitchen, he put the laptop case down and went about removing the laptop. "I was working the night Jed Johnson was killed."

"Why haven't you gone to the police?"

He booted up the laptop. "This is Cold Plains, Ms. Johnson. Sometimes the cops can't be trusted."

"I don't understand." Then she took a closer look at the laptop. As the screen came to life, she recognized the background picture. "That's Jed's laptop!"

He opened Windows Explorer and stopped to face her. "Ma'am, I could be killed for what I'm about to show you. I didn't have to come here, but I did. After I read that article, I knew I had to."

"Where did you get that laptop?"

He hesitated. "I stole it."

"From Jed's hotel room?"

He nodded. "I'm the one who called in his murder. I'm the one who found him. Now, I know how bad this is going to sound, but I frequently watch guests and find the ones who have money. I was going to wait until Mr. Johnson left his room, but one time I walked by and the door was open. I saw this here laptop and decided to take it. I put it in my car before the cops arrived."

"You stole…" She gaped at him. "How could you? Steal from a dead person?"

"I don't expect you to understand. Times have been hard for me. Stealing's kept food on my family's table." He faced the computer and shook his head. "I've given this a lot of thought and I just can't keep this a secret. I've got to do what's right."

Gemma normally wasn't the kind to forgive anyone for taking what didn't belong to them, but this man had an odd sort of honor about him. She watched as he opened a video file.

A dim clip began to play. Jed's face appeared. Part of a bed was visible behind him. Some closed drapes. His hotel room. A knock brought him to his feet and he disappeared from the camera's view. Muffled voices followed and then a hard thud. After a few minutes of shuffling, she glanced at David.

"Keep watching."

She did. The silhouette of a man appeared briefly, and then vanished. Seconds later, David appeared and the video clip ended when he closed the computer.

"Who was that?"

"I don't know."

"Did you see him?"

"No."

"We have to go to the police."

"No. No police. Please. I came to do what's right. I beg you not to reveal my identity to anyone. You can call the cops as soon as I leave."

"You stole my ex-husband's laptop."

His head bowed as though he was gathering his wits. "Ms. Johnson, you may not know the kind of people who are running this town, so I'm going to warn you. When this video file is discovered, some very bad people are going to want to stop it from reaching anyone who can identify the killer. I risked my life coming here."

Gemma stared at him. Everything Ford said must be true. She could no longer deny any of it. "Samuel?"

"He's behind it all. The disappearances. The murders. That Jane Doe case Ford is investigating? I'll bet he's got something to do with it."

Rubbing her arms, Gemma wandered to her back patio door and looked outside. Just when she thought she was safe again, this happened.

"You'd better go," she said.

"I need your word, Ms Johnson."

"I won't reveal your identity."

After a long sigh of relief, he said, "Thank you." A few seconds later, she heard the front door close.

Facing the laptop again, she replayed the video. She still couldn't see enough of the man to identify him. There was only one thing she could do. Only one person she could turn to. Unfortunately, he was also the one person she shouldn't be close to right now.

When Gemma opened the door, Ford devoured the sight of her in a denim dress and no shoes. Her dark hair flowed over her shoulders and her beautiful brown eyes roamed all over him, pausing on his badge before falling to the carry-on-sized suitcase beside him on her front porch.

After receiving her call, he'd known he wouldn't be leaving her alone. Once word got out that there was a recording of Jed's murder, Grayson would have his henchmen combing the town for it. That was his reasoning. His heart had another story. It didn't help that she had accurately assessed him after Grayson's party. He was afraid of what she meant to him. He was afraid she'd mean too much if he allowed it. Fortunately, his heart didn't make his decisions for him.

Wordlessly, she made room for him to enter. He put his luggage just inside the door and went into the kitchen where the laptop was. After watching the clip, he had to agree with Gemma. The image of the man was too dark.

He shut the computer down and faced her. "Why don't you tell me who gave it to you?" She'd refused to on the phone.

"I can't."

"Why not?"

"He asked me not to."

"A man steals a laptop from a dead man and you want to protect him?"

She explained how David Retting had entered the room and found Jed. He'd taken the computer to sell it so he could feed his family. "And now he's afraid."

Ford didn't care if it was her ex-husband's computer, stealing was wrong.

"He didn't have to come forward," she argued.

No, he didn't.

"It was the desk clerk at the Stillwater," Ford said. "That's who took the computer." It wasn't that hard to figure out.

At her startled look, he added, "He called in the murder."

"Oh." Warmth danced in her eyes.

"What's he afraid of?"

"Samuel."

"He's afraid Grayson will find out he had the recording and gave it to you?"

She nodded.

Something was different about her. She wasn't defending Grayson anymore. "Do you believe him?"

"Yes."

Hearing her say that should make him feel a lot better. It did, but not in a way that made him comfortable. She was on his side now. No longer would he have to butt heads with her regarding Grayson's cult. Instead, he'd have to fight even harder not to touch her.

"It would probably be best if you continue to behave the way you have," he said. "The hotel clerk is right. We don't want anyone to find out about the recording."

"Okay."

"Keep going to the seminars."

"What if Samuel invites me to another party?"

As much as he hated the idea, he said, "You'll go. Don't even tell Lacy. By now you must know she's one of them."

"I haven't seen a *D* on her hip and she hasn't said she's gotten one."

"I know she's your friend, Gemma, but you can't trust her. You have to assume her first allegiance is to Samuel Grayson."

Reluctantly, she nodded. "What are we going to do with the recording?"

"I know someone who might be able to help us."

All they had to do was leave town without anyone knowing. Or following. It would keep him busy and his mind off Gemma. For now. Living with her again didn't fill him with an abundance of confidence.

Chapter 7

Dillon threw a small pebble at the second-floor window of Hallie's house. The middle of July had brought dry heat to Cold Plains, but it cooled off at night. When no one appeared, he threw two more. He'd always wanted to do this. Hallie appeared in the lit window. She opened it a crack. "What are you doing?"

"Want to go to a party?"

"Are you nuts?"

"Grayson reserved the bar at the Stillwater. My parents are there." His mom hadn't been drinking the way she used to. He'd noticed other changes in her, too. Like the way she stood up to his dad more. His dad was a lost cause but there was still hope for his mom.

"Wait there." Hallie disappeared and a few minutes later she emerged through the front door of her grandmother's house.

"My grandmother is already asleep."

"Good." Dillon looked across the street at Gemma's house.

Ford's SUV was parked in the driveway behind her car. There were lights on inside but no sign of Ford. He didn't want to be caught going to the inn.

He started driving. "So, when are you going to tell me why you're spying on Samuel?"

As always she didn't respond, just looked forward as he drove.

"Or is it Bo Fargo you're after?"

"I'm not after him."

He smiled because she'd given herself away. She wasn't after Fargo; she had other motives, like watching him. Just like he was watching Grayson.

He heard her sigh. Several seconds passed. "He refused to help my grandmother and me when we came to him about my father." She paused. "My father disappeared a few months ago."

"What do you mean he disappeared?"

"He moved me and my grandmother here. She lived with us. He wouldn't say why we moved here. But as soon as we settled in, weird things started happening."

"Was he a Devotee?"

"No. He was the opposite. He despised Samuel and his followers. He was fairly vocal about it, too. He received several threats before he disappeared."

"They chased him out of town?"

"He would never leave me and my grandmother here. Something happened to him and I think Bo Fargo knows exactly what that is."

"What makes you think that?"

"He wouldn't do anything to help us find him. He claimed my dad told him he was going to take a trip to Australia and that maybe he decided not to come back."

Dillon parked his truck along the street in front of the woodsy landscaping of Stillwater Inn. It was a nice building and location, but it could also be in a horror movie. Too many dark places to hide outside. Dim lighting inside. Stillwater Inn…creepy.

"I've heard that happens a lot in this town."

"I need to know where my father is."

Her earnestness was a dart hitting the center of what drove him. "Well, let's go join the party, then."

She got out of his truck when he did. He locked it and walked around to her.

"They're going to kick us out," Hallie said as she walked beside him toward the inn. "We weren't invited."

"They won't even know we're there."

"What if they do?"

"We'll say we're with my parents."

"They won't believe us."

"Stop worrying so much."

She looked around. "Why are we here anyway? Nobody's going to do anything in front of a bunch of people."

"I need to make sure my mother is all right."

She turned to him and he saw the warm admiration in her eyes. She liked his reason.

"I can also see who's here. Who my parents talk to, who Samuel talks to."

"Bo Fargo?" The name rolled off her tongue with a sneer.

"Yes. Him, too."

Dillon took Hallie's hand, glad she trusted him now. She didn't pull away and the tiny smile told him she liked the gesture. Up the stairs to the porch, he opened the door for her and they entered.

Inside the foyer, a banner hung above the heavy wooden double doors of the bar. Health and Prosperity Hour. An interesting twist on a regular happy hour. The doors were open to a loud throng of women in cocktail dresses and men in suits. He and Hallie were in jeans.

"This is never going to work," Hallie said.

"Come on." He led her to a vacant table, tucked back in

the corner and adjacent to the doors. The dim lighting would help conceal them.

"Tonic?"

Dillon looked up at the waiter and shared a quick glance with Hallie. She shrugged and nodded. Dillon took two glasses and handed her one. The waiter moved on.

Dillon clinked Hallie's glass. "To meeting you."

She smiled. "To meeting you."

Her green eyes twinkled and her thick brown hair glimmered in the soft light.

Back to the reason he'd come here, he searched the room and found his parents. His mom was drinking a bottle of water. That stunned him for a second. She was at a party and drinking water. He looked around again. Everyone was drinking water. Was his mom doing the same because his dad had ordered her to or was she finally starting to listen to Dillon? The bottle she held wasn't just any kind of water. It was Samuel's tonic water. He hoped she drank it just to fit in and didn't buy all the crap that jerk fed everyone. Though she appeared a tad detached, she was holding up fine. His dad was immersed in a conversation with another man.

A little to the left, the crowd parted and he saw Samuel Grayson standing with his second in command, Wade Herrington, and that goon who'd kicked him out of the inn the last time he was here. Wade was speaking to Samuel in what appeared to be a low-volume discussion. Samuel nodded and Wade wandered away. He was a tall, lean man with blond hair and an unsmiling face. Dillon's mom had told him that Wade ran the community center for Samuel.

Samuel turned to the goon and said something that made him nod. Just before the crowd closed over Dillon's view of them, the goon glanced over at him.

"Damn."

"What?"

"We've been spotted."

* * *

"Gemma." Ford leaned over her bed and touched her shoulder, trying not to let the sight of her half covered by the blanket seduce him. He'd managed to keep his hands off her throughout the evening. It helped that she'd been distant. He didn't want to ask why because he didn't want her to tell him that it was his own distance that bothered her. One kiss and they'd be burning up the stairs again.

Her eyes popped open.

"Sorry," he said. "I had to wake you."

She sprang up to a sitting position. "What's wrong? What happened?"

"Get dressed. You have to come with me."

"What? Where?" She blinked tiredly and pushed her messy hair off her face, messy hair that he yearned to have his fingers in just now.

"I can't leave you here alone. You go where I go, and that's the Stillwater Inn."

"Why do you have to go there?"

"We. I got a call about a disturbance at the Stillwater Inn." He pulled the covers off her.

"Hey."

"Come on. Get dressed. I'll wait for you downstairs."

Grumbling under her breath, she got out of bed and went into her walk-in closet, giving him a nice view of her body shimmering in a thin, knee-length nightgown before he could turn to leave the room. Sexy and petite, she was adorable when she was awakened from a dead sleep and forced to get moving. He wished he could hold her in bed while she fell back asleep.

He went downstairs and waited, only to be rewarded again when she appeared in a dark blue cotton tank that hinted to stiff nipples—she'd gone braless—and denim shorts that showcased her legs.

"Ready." Gemma yawned as she headed for the door, oblivious to what she was doing to him.

Ford fought to keep from looking at her all the way to the inn. She caught him a couple of times, especially once she stopped yawning. Maybe that's why she stopped yawning.

He spotted Bo out in the street, next to an older blue-and-white Chevy pickup truck, and was glad to have something else to occupy his mind. There were two kids standing between two big men who had *henchmen* written all over them. He'd seen them with Samuel before. He'd also seen the kids. Dillon and Hallie.

Ford parked and he and Gemma walked toward the group. Bo looked speculatively from Gemma to him.

Ford ignored him. "What's the problem?"

"We caught these two out here drinking," Bo said.

"That's a lie," Dillon retorted. "We were inside and these two dragged us out here."

"This was in the truck." One of the henchmen held up a six-pack of beer with two cans missing.

"They planted that in there!" Dillon protested. Beside him, Hallie's eyes spat darts of anger at Bo and she folded her arms.

"Arrest them," Bo ordered. "Maybe after a night in jail they'll rethink underage drinking from now on."

"We weren't underage drinking," Hallie argued. "That's just another one of his lies! Just like he lied about looking for my father."

Ford studied Bo, who gave nothing away. It was pointless to question him or the henchmen right now. They'd all lie. Hallie was right about that.

"Grayson having a party?" he asked Bo, nodding toward the inn.

"Health and Prosperity Hour," Dillon sneered.

Ford hid a smirk. Kind of like happy hour for health nuts?

"It's an adult party. These two shouldn't be here, and they

made a mistake drinking in the truck." Bo turned threat-eningly to the two kids. "One they're going to learn not to repeat."

Why had Dillon and Hallie shown up here tonight? The two had been together the night of Gemma's second attack, and they'd been together on the Fourth of July. Were they just two kids out for a fun night of drinking as Bo claimed or was it something else? Given their proximity to Samuel and Bo every time he saw them, he doubted this was a simple case of young love.

"Why don't you two come with me," he told them.

"What?" Dillon raged. "That's so unfair! You're actually going to listen to that puke?"

Bo took an intimidating step toward Dillon. "I'll arrest you myself if you don't watch it."

Planting a hand on his superior's chest, Ford stopped him. "I'll take care of it."

Gemma took Hallie's hand. "Come on. It's okay."

Seeing Hallie following Gemma, Dillon looked at Ford, hesitating.

"Take them in," Bo demanded.

Casting a glare back at Bo, Dillon walked angrily toward Ford's Escalade. Ford followed without cuffing either teen-ager, not caring what Bo thought.

When the kids were belted in the back, Ford drove away from the inn.

"You're actually going to arrest us?" Dillon demanded. "I thought you were different from the rest."

"We'll go somewhere we can talk."

With that, Dillon relaxed against the seat and Ford drove back to Gemma's house. When he pulled into the driveway, he received curious looks from all the occupants.

Catching Gemma's glance, he tried to reassure her. "Trust me on this."

On the way to the front door, Hallie looked back at her

grandmother's house. Dillon put his hand on her back, as though keeping her from trying to bolt.

Inside Gemma's living room, Ford took out his notebook and a pen. "Sit down."

Hallie sat on the sofa across from the two blue-and-green wingback chairs and Dillon sat next to her. Gemma went into the kitchen.

"Start from the top," Ford said. "Tell me what happened."

Hallie glanced at Dillon, who nodded and turned back to Ford.

"Why didn't you arrest us?" he asked.

"I don't always do what Bo tells me. I do what's right. Now start talking, or I will arrest you."

"We went there to make sure Dillon's mom was okay," Hallie said.

"I've been following her," Dillon added.

Ford tried to remember if he'd seen Dillon's parents in Grayson's tent on the Fourth of July and couldn't. "Why have you been doing that?"

Gemma appeared with four colorful glasses and a matching pitcher full of water. Putting them on the coffee table, she handed one to Ford. "Thanks." He put the glass down on a table beside one of her pretty chairs.

"Because I saw a *D* tattooed on my dad's hip and I'm worried he'll hurt my mom." Dillon said, taking a glass from Gemma.

"Has he hurt her in the past?"

"Yeah. He beats her. But he's got her too scared to do anything about it."

Gemma slowed in her movements as she handed Hallie a glass next. News of any woman being beaten by her husband wouldn't go over well with her.

"Your mother doesn't want to be a part of what your dad is doing?" Ford continued his questioning.

Dillon shook his head. "No way. He forces her to do everything."

"And when she refuses he gets physical?"

"Yes. Mostly he slaps her but lately he's been getting worse. Shoving. Punching."

Looking down, clearly bothered by Dillon's revelation, Gemma sipped her water.

"Has she had to go to the hospital?"

"No."

"And no police."

"No."

So there was no record of the abuse, and her son had taken it upon himself to protect her. No son should have to do that.

"Were your parents at the inn tonight?"

"Yes."

"And the beer?"

"Those apes planted it in my truck!" Dillon burst out.

Ford believed that. "Why did you take Hallie there? You have a reason to want to keep tabs on your mother, but why involve Hallie in something that could potentially be dangerous?"

Hallie didn't answer and Dillon's quick glance over at her alerted him.

"You and your grandmother are new to town, isn't that right, Hallie?"

"Yes."

"Why did you say that Bo lied about looking for your father? Is he missing?"

She didn't respond right away, flashing a nervous look at Dillon.

"It's okay, Hallie," Gemma said. "You can tell him."

"Go ahead. Tell him," Dillon encouraged.

Slowly, Hallie turned back to Ford. "About four years ago, my dad was having an affair with a woman who was from

Cold Plains, though he didn't know it at the time. She disappeared, and he couldn't find her."

Ford's alertness sharpened tenfold. "Four years ago?" Jane Doe had been murdered then.

Hallie nodded. "About a year ago, my dad found out she was from Cold Plains. And then he learned that Samuel Grayson was running a cult here. He wondered if she knew and had a reason to come back. He moved us here so he could do his own poking around. Samuel must have caught him, because he disappeared just like the woman."

"I didn't see the Missing Persons report." Had Bo tried to cover it up? "When did he disappear?"

"Three months ago."

"Who was the woman?" Could it be his Jane Doe? He dug into his shirt pocket for the computer-enhanced photo he always carried with him.

"He never revealed her name. Everything I'm telling you he told only my grandmother. He was too afraid of anyone else getting hurt, and he kept his affair secret to protect me. My mother died shortly before he met this woman and he thought I'd be upset."

"He didn't tell your grandmother the woman's name?"

Hallie shook her head. "To avoid any connection between his family and her."

"Have you ever seen the woman?"

"Grandma showed me a picture. It was the only picture my dad kept of her."

"Is this the woman?" He showed her the photo.

Hallie leaned forward. "Yes, I think that's her." She looked up. "Who is she?"

"I don't know her name." And neither did Hallie. But she'd just given him the biggest lead he'd gotten so far. A lover. She must have run away from Grayson long before she was killed. But somehow their paths had crossed again. Four years ago. Why? Had Grayson been searching for her? Had she unearthed something about him? Something that threatened him enough to kill her?

"Did you file a Missing Persons report?" he asked.

"Yes." Now she sounded angry. "But we were forced to go through Bo Fargo."

Bo *had* covered it up. "I'll take care of that."

Dillon elbowed her with a smile, a silent I-told-you-we-could-trust-him communication.

"How did the two of you link up?" Ford asked.

"We bumped into each other at the inn," Dillon replied.

"The Stillwater?"

"Yeah. I followed my dad. He met Grayson and some other people there. Bo Fargo and a few of his thugs. I heard my dad tell my mother that Wade Herrington would be there. She didn't go with him, but he sounded excited to meet the man."

"Who is Wade Herrington?" Gemma asked.

"Grayson's right hand," Ford answered. "He runs the community center and other things less visible to the public."

"Why was your dad excited to meet him?" she asked Dillon.

"He's working his way up the whacko food chain, I guess. Wade is important to Samuel. Maybe my dad wants to be important, too."

Or was he taking orders from Herrington?

"I also saw Lacy Matthews at the inn with her boyfriend," Dillon added.

"Alan?" Gemma breathed anxiously.

"Alan Chapman?" Ford asked. He'd seen the man with Grayson, and also one of his henchmen.

"He's a big dude," Dillon said. "Like my dad."

"If Lacy was there, she wasn't involved in anything they were doing," Gemma said.

Ford didn't think it was a coincidence Grayson had been meeting at the inn around the time of Jed's murder. It would place one of his goons at the inn with an alibi. Ballsy, but that was the way Grayson operated.

"Tell no one about this conversation." Ford looked at Hallie. "If you want to find your father, and you—" he looked at Dillon "—if you want to help your mother, you'll both be quiet. And you'll stay away from Samuel Grayson and anyone associated with him. Understood?"

Hallie nodded. And Dillon said, "Yeah."

"No more going to his parties."

Both teenagers nodded this time.

"No more sneaking around of any kind. You'll be in your houses before dark until I say it's safe to do otherwise. Understood?"

"What about my—"

"I'll watch over your mother," Ford interrupted. He had to make sure these two did not try to take on an investigation that was far, far, above their heads. The last thing he wanted to hear about was the disappearance of two innocent teenagers.

Late the next morning, Gemma watched Ford standing at the kitchen table in front of his laptop, wondering if now was a good time to tell him her period was a week late and she was worried. She didn't know him well enough to gauge how he'd react. She only knew he'd lost everyone he'd loved and had a barrier thicker than the Earth's mantle around his heart. Not to mention the complication of Jed's murder and now the discovery of Jane Doe's lover.

After they'd dropped Dillon off last night, they'd driven Hallie home and questioned her grandmother. She hadn't revealed anything more than her granddaughter had. Ford had searched Felix Taylor's things, but there again, nothing had turned up. She could tell he was frustrated.

"What are you doing?" she asked.

"Sending a message to someone."

She had wireless hookup in the house and he must have found it. "Who?"

Stopping in the middle of typing, he looked up and didn't answer. Didn't he trust her enough to tell her? She thought they'd crossed that boundary.

"Someone who might be able to help find Felix. Dead or alive."

He wasn't going to tell her. He may have gotten her pregnant but he didn't trust her with details of his investigation. Or maybe it had more to do with the way he closed his heart off to her. Confiding in her might make him feel too intimate with her. She wasn't someone special to him, and he would keep it that way.

Going back into the living room, she sat on the sofa, dejected. When he finished, he came into the living room and sat beside her, putting his arm over her shoulders along the back of the sofa. Casual. Like they were buddies.

"I have to keep some things secret, Gemma. It's crucial to the investigation."

Not as crucial as it was to guard his heart.

He touched her chin with his fingers and moved her head so she had to look at him. "Is something else wrong?"

"No." Just that she thought she was pregnant and he wouldn't be there for her.

"It seems like something's bothering you."

Oh, my God. He could tell?

"You mean like being accused of murder?" She smiled with her attempt at humor.

He grinned back, looking sexy as hell. He glided his hand along her jaw, caressing her skin with his thumb. And just like that he had her insides going haywire.

This was going to lead to trouble. Sweet, agonizing trouble.

When he dipped his head, she lifted hers. Their mouths were oh so close. Instantaneous passion erupted. He kissed her. Sitting side by side made access cumbersome. He leaned toward her, guiding her back onto the sofa, and then he was on top of her. Their kisses grew searching and ardent.

Gemma arched for him. He groaned from deep down and reached for the hem of her shirt.

He might have already gotten her pregnant. He didn't even know that. The idea of him fathering her baby became an aphrodisiac, an irrational one, but a delicious one nonetheless.

Ford's phone went off. Sanity crashed down on her. What was she thinking? She stopped kissing him back and opened her eyes. His opened shortly thereafter and sanity began to filter back to him, too.

Swearing, he got up. "I'm sorry."

"Stop apologizing," she hissed, "You're not the only one who was ready to start tearing clothes off."

He stood there catching his breath, at a loss as much as she was. His cell phone kept ringing.

"At least we didn't do it on the stairs again."

"The couch wouldn't have been much of an improvement."

The thought of making it to her bed gave her a shudder, and not from dread. That's what scared her.

That and the prospect of telling him she was pregnant. Never in her life had she yearned to have her period more than now.

Ford's phone stopped ringing just as he picked it up. He frowned when he saw who had called.

"Bo Fargo?"

He looked up at her as though surprised she'd guessed.

"He must have just found out I didn't arrest those kids."

Gemma hoped that was all he'd found out.

Chapter 8

Gemma followed Ford across the parking lot to the entrance of the Cold Plains Police Department. The building was non-descript compared to the community center. It suited Ford. She could see him running this operation, with Bo out of the way. Through the lobby, she walked beside him down a long hallway adorned with pictures of Main Street, the community center and the famed creek that supposedly produced such magical water. They passed a copy machine and a meeting room before reaching a waiting area with an administrative assistant's cubicle and two offices.

Bo sat behind a shiny mahogany desk in the larger one. Seeing them approach, he stood, liquid blue eyes rising below the reflective gleam of his balding head. Gemma entered the office and stopped beside Ford. Bo's gaze fixed on her before pinning him with reproach.

"Still protecting her?" he asked, standing to his full height behind the desk.

"What's so important that you couldn't talk on the phone?" Ford replied.

The snub didn't go over well with the Chief of Police. His balding head left nothing to distract from the angry furrow marring his high forehead. He moved around his desk to stand in front of Ford, who didn't even flinch.

"Why did you bring her here?"

"You didn't say this was a confidential meeting."

"I'm getting tired of your attitude, McCall."

"Just doing my job."

"Your job is to do what I tell you. Last night I told you to arrest those kids. Where are they?"

"Probably at home. Sleeping in."

Gemma watched Bo struggle with his temper and then leash it in. "Why didn't you arrest them like I told you to?"

Why was he so bent on arresting two innocent teenagers? Had he intended to supply a lesson? For their good or for his own agenda? Did he want to scare them so they stopped showing up wherever Dillon's dad went, which also happened to be where Bo and Samuel went?

"After I questioned them it became obvious we didn't have cause."

"If I say there's cause, there's cause. Alcohol was found in the boy's vehicle."

"Dillon didn't put it there, and neither he nor the girl were drinking."

"Why were they there?" Bo demanded.

Ford's hesitation was calculated. Gemma could see it in his confident eyes.

"Dillon believes his father is one of Grayson's Devotees," he finally said. "And Hallie's father had an affair with our Jane Doe."

The detonation of that bomb wiped Bo's aura of power away. Gemma wondered why Ford was telling the man all this.

"I thought I told you to stop investigating that case?"

Again, Ford remained silent. The message was clear, however. Ford was not going to stop investigating the Jane Doe case, and he was taunting Bo with his newest lead.

"Was the girl able to identify the woman in your computer-enhanced photo?"

"Yes, but she didn't know her name."

That relaxed Bo. His gaze drifted to Gemma. "Why are you here with Ford?"

She glanced uncertainly from him to Ford.

"She won't be out of my sight until Jed Johnson's murder investigation is closed," Ford answered.

"That's going above and beyond. And how accommodating for her to agree to let you stay with her."

Ford allowed that comment to pass.

"As long as you don't let your personal affairs get in the way, and you start keeping me informed of your activities, that's okay. You should have called me about Dillon."

"I'll do my best, Chief."

And that was as much as Bo would get.

"Samuel would be real disappointed if you turn out to be anything he doesn't expect." He turned to Gemma. "You, too."

"Don't worry about me, Mr. Fargo," Gemma said sweetly. "I have tremendous respect for Samuel and what he means to this town, and to me. I would never do anything to jeopardize that."

A shady smile inched up on Bo's mouth as he understood her subtle meaning. Samuel didn't tolerate violence, and she hadn't killed her ex-husband. "I'm happy to hear that. Now if you can just keep my second-in-command in line."

"He manages that all on his own."

"I'm not so sure." He turned to Ford. "I spoke with a friend over at the McMurrow Forensics Lab. Seems you dropped off a laptop to one of the technicians there."

Gemma stiffened. How had he discovered that so fast? He must have friends all over the place keeping an eye out for anything suspicious. To protect Samuel. Judging from Ford's careful silence and lack of reaction, he'd been aware of that for a while. He didn't even seem surprised.

"Why didn't you tell me about it?" Bo asked.

"Why are you worried?"

"I'm worried?" Clearly Bo thought Ford was the one who should be worried. "Where did the laptop come from?"

Was Bo baiting him or did he already know the answer to that question?

"Someone who wishes to remain anonymous gave it to me."

Bo's now very eerie gaze turned to Gemma. She moved closer to Ford, hooking her arm with his.

"Then that person will remain anonymous. Now tell me who it was."

"Sorry, I can't do that."

"Why not?"

Ford gave no reply.

A heavy veil of distrust blanketed the office.

"Tell me who gave you the laptop, Ford." Bo's demanding tone would have made Gemma crumble.

Ford didn't budge.

Bo moved closer to him in what must have been intended to intimidate his subordinate. "You're walking a very thin line, McCall. I suggest you think carefully which side you fall on."

"You know which side I fall on. It's the side I've always fallen on. I suggest you take your own advice, Bo."

Ford fell on the side of the law, and Bo was precariously teetering to the opposite. Ford had just told his own boss that he'd go against him if he could prove where his loyalties really lay.

"You have no idea what you're doing."

"Ford, let's go," Gemma urged, then gave her farewel. "Bo."

He looked from her to Ford, who let her tug him toward the door.

"Remember what I said about keeping me informed of your activities," Bo called.

Ford didn't stop or turn around, much to Gemma's relief. Not that she didn't like what he'd done. She loved it. His fearless confidence and defense of the law was stronger than ever. He never backed down from the right cause.

Gemma swooned.

Reaching his SUV, she wondered if something was wrong with her. His lawman attributes sure did electrify her. She blamed her ordeal with Jed. It had made her weak. Made her judgment bad. Right now she had a weakness for lawmen. Lawmen didn't beat up their women. Not lawmen like Ford, anyway. He was her protector. Her lover…

Just watching him drive made her wild for him. His hands. His arms. His shoulders. That handsome profile. Big. Strong. Lawman. Father of her baby…

She rubbed her thighs. Damn if she didn't love that idea.

Ford saw her rubbing her thighs and glanced at her in question. She stopped and pretended not to notice.

The next morning, Gemma went with Ford to the forensics laboratory, sixty minutes outside of town. He walked beside her on the way to the front doors of the concrete-and-steel structure with dark-tinted windows and a flat roof. A few pine trees and blue spruce broke up the yellowing grass. Other than that, it was plain and simple. He held the door open for her and a security guard looked up from his computer screen.

The guard broke into a smile when he recognized Ford.

"Deputy McCall." He stood up.

"Patrick." Ford stopped in front of the desk with Gemma.

Then the guard's friendly smile vanished. "You're here to see Michael Harris, aren't you."

"Yes." Judging from Patrick's grim face, this wasn't going to be good news.

"I hate to be the one to tell you this. He was strangled to death the night before last. Police say some type of rope was used and he was hit over the head first."

A tiny gasp came from Gemma.

"The night before last?"

"Yes."

Bo must have known and hadn't told them. He'd probably had something to do with the murder. "Any leads?"

"None. Lab was ransacked, but nothing appears to be missing. Everybody's talking about it. Who would want to kill Michael? He didn't have any enemies."

Ford had asked Michael not to tell anyone about the laptop and to carefully guard what he found in the video and hard drive. Somehow someone had discovered what he had. Someone close to Bo. "Can we take a look inside the lab?"

The guard glanced around him. "I'm not supposed to let anyone in there. The place is on high alert. Michael was a good man. He lived a quiet life. For someone to kill him…"

"I need to get into that lab."

The guard glanced around again. A worker passed and disappeared behind a secure door.

"Please. We really need to get into that lab," Gemma pleaded. She had a lot to lose if the laptop and any trace of the recording were gone.

Ford took out his wallet and counted five twenties, handing them to the guard.

The guard looked from the cash to Ford and then Gemma, hesitating.

"Please," Gemma repeated.

Ford took out another five twenties. He'd made sure he had a lot of cash before he'd come here, planning for the worst. He had befriended Patrick for a reason. A security guard could come in handy when you least expected it, especially when Grayson's evil arms reached this far away from Cold Plains.

Patrick took the money. "All right, but you'll have to find your own way in."

Ford gave him a single nod. "Thanks."

He and Gemma moved away from the counter just as a worker headed for the secure door, oblivious to his surroundings, bored and unenthusiastic. Taking Gemma's hand, Ford walked faster. The worker reached the door and used his badge to open it. Ford caught the door and entered behind him. The man didn't even look back.

Ford was familiar with this building. Michael's lab was straight down this hall. If he was going to get in, he'd need a badge. He knew exactly which one he was going to take, too. When Bo had said he had a friend here, Ford had had a very good idea who that could be. Passing Michael's lab, he headed for the executive offices. When he found the Vice President of Security's office, he was pleased to see the door open and Galen Steele sitting inside. Michael had mentioned that he'd seen Bo meeting with him. Ford hadn't thought it would be an issue, since Michael wouldn't have told Galen about the laptop. But somehow, he was sure, the VP had found out.

"Wait right here," he told Gemma.

"What are you—"

He put his hands on her waist to stop her, and experienced a moment of awareness of that touch. Her lips parted and her light brown eyes looked up at him. "Wait right here," he said.

She nodded a couple of times. "Just hurry."

He went into the office and shut the door. Galen had already looked up from his computer.

"What are you doing here?"

Galen knew who Ford was. "Bo Fargo sent me."

The man stared warily at him. "What for?"

"Insurance. He wasn't planning on having to clean up after you."

Galen's eyes widened in a flash before calming. "Hey, if you think I had anything to do with Michael's murder, I didn't."

Ford walked around the desk to loom over the man. "Bo doesn't like messes."

"He asked for information, I gave it to him, that's it. The rest is his problem," Galen said.

Just as he'd gambled, Bo hadn't told the security VP that Ford had given the laptop to Michael, only that Michael had it.

Ford popped the man's temple with his fist. Galen staggered off his chair and fell to his hands and knees, trying to crawl away. Slipping out his gun, Ford stepped around the office chair and then hit the back of Galen's head. He flattened onto the floor and didn't move. He'd be out long enough.

Ford pulled the lanyard and the badge clipped to it from it from the executive's neck and left the office, shutting the door behind him. He saw Gemma's big, round eyes darting one way and then another. She wasn't accustomed to this type of investigative work. Not that he went around slugging people and knocking them out to get what he needed as a rule.

"Stay behind me." He put the lanyard around his neck, making sure it was backward, the name and picture facing his chest, and started for Michael's lab.

A worker in a lab coat passed them without looking too closely at them. Another worker passed and glanced down at Ford's badge. Ford feigned nonchalance. The worker passed without issue, not seeing Gemma enough to notice she wore no identification.

At the door of Michael's lab, Ford swiped Galen's badge. The door clicked and he pushed it open, entering ahead of Gemma. Her steps slowed as she took in the expanse of equipment. Tables lined the walls and two more were pushed together in the center of the room. Gadgets and computers littered their surfaces. Cabinets and equipment filled in the spaces between.

Ford searched the surfaces first, then had to break into a locked cabinet. He already knew Michael stored his most valuable hard drives in here. Jed's laptop was nowhere to be found.

Cursing, he shut the cabinet door.

"It's not here," Gemma said.

She sounded scared. The laptop would have cleared her of any guilt and now it was gone, likely in Bo's hands, never to be seen again.

"Come on. Let's go search Michael's house."

Retracing their steps toward the exit, Ford kept a careful watch for detection.

"You. Stop right there!"

Gemma inhaled a startled breath as they looked back and saw a security guard holding a cell phone. He wasn't armed.

Galen must have been found.

Grabbing Gemma's hand, Ford ran for the door leading to the lobby.

"Block the exits!" he heard the guard shout into the phone.

He shoved the lobby door open and saw Patrick frantically talking to two other men. A door across from the lobby swung open and another guard rushed through. This one was armed.

"Stop them!"

The unarmed guard entered the lobby, still talking into the phone.

Damn. Having to pull Gemma along with him, he moved closer to the armed guard.

"I said stop!"

"Mr. McCall..." Patrick warned.

Ford slipped out his pistol as he drew closer to the armed guard, stopping just a few feet away.

"Give me the gun." The guard held out one of his hands.

Hearing the guard who'd caught them in the hall move up behind him and Gemma, Ford held up his pistol. The armed guard tentatively moved closer, exactly as Ford hoped. He lunged, hitting the guard's gun, deflecting his aim while he punched him hard enough to make him bow forward. Quickly maneuvering behind him, Ford hooked his arm around the man's neck and pressed his pistol against his temple.

"Drop it," he told the other guard.

After a bit of hesitation, the guard dropped his gun. Patrick sank down onto his chair. The two men standing next to him didn't move.

"Gemma, go through the doors."

Her fast breathing belied her courage. She walked slowly backward toward the door.

Ford backed up after her, using the guard as a hostage. At the door, he pushed the guard and used his foot to kick him back into the lobby.

Running through the door, he grabbed Gemma's hand and ran with her to his SUV.

They scrambled in and he wheeled the Escalade around and gave it full power. Zigzagging through a neighborhood, he slowed long enough to use the computer attached to his dash to look up Michael Harris's home address.

"Do you think we'll find the laptop there?"

"If it's not there, we'll know that Bo has it."

In his rearview mirror, he saw the security guard with the cell phone, holding it to his head and talking rapidly. He'd gotten Ford's plate number. That didn't matter. Bo already knew Ford had brought the laptop to Michael without telling him. They were now playing a very dangerous game. His biggest concern was for Gemma. Bo could fire him, or even send one of Samuel's henchmen after him. Gemma would be caught in the crossfire. Or maybe she was caught anyway.

Jed's killer had planted her bracelet next to his body to take the heat off himself. The laptop threatened exposure. And Bo was at the center of it all, doing Samuel's bidding. But what did Samuel want from Gemma? Would he let the murder go unsolved? Welcome Gemma into his circle? Or would he drive her out of town, or worse, kill her?

Samuel would have to get past Ford first.

The front door of Michael's house was locked, but the back door wasn't. He slid it open and was relieved to see nothing disturbed. No one had been here. That meant Bo had the laptop.

Taking Gemma's hand, he led her through the house to Michael's office. He'd been here a few times before, whenever he had something he needed Michael to look at without Bo's knowledge.

Inside the office, headlights from the street flashed through the window. Ford pulled Gemma out of the stream of light. She landed against him and he held her around her waist. Once again she looked up at him with her lips parted and her eyes inquisitive and hot.

"Woman, you're killing me."

She stepped back. "You keep touching me."

Taking in her small form and round, perky breasts, he turned in frustration and went to the desk, booting the computer. Gemma put her hands on the back of the chair and watched over his head.

The computer was password protected. Gemma started opening a drawer to his right and he opened the one on the left. She found a small notebook and flipped through the pages.

She stopped and pushed her forefinger into his biceps, showing him a page.

The words *For Ford* were handwritten there. And then a word followed by four numbers. The password. There was something on this computer.

His heart picking up speed, he tore the page out and typed in the password, then searched through folders and files.

"Open his email," Gemma said. "Maybe he emailed himself the video file."

"Good thinking." He didn't think Michael would have done that, not after their conversation when he'd dropped off the laptop. But maybe he'd sent something else. Some kind of clue.

There was an email from his work account six deep in the inbox. A forwarded message.

"That's from Lacy to Jed. That's Jed's email address." Her voice held a tremor.

"Yeah." He opened the email.

Gemma stood straighter, resting her hand on the back of the office chair to read the email. In it, Lacy warned Jed to leave town before he was killed. "Oh, my God."

"How did she get his email address?"

A moment went by while she thought. "I showed her some emails he sent to me before he came to Cold Plains."

"He sent you emails?"

"Yes, things like, 'I miss you, come home,' and 'Why did you have to do this to us?' Disturbing. Stalker emails. That's why I showed them to Lacy. I wanted to see what she thought."

"What did she say?"

"She agreed they were creepy and told me not to respond to any of them."

"Did you?"

"No."

Why did she warn him to leave town? What reason would she have? Why care about a man who hurt her friend? Would a true Devotee do that? If she was beginning to see through

Grayson's deception, knew what happened to anyone who didn't fit in…

Maybe she simply didn't want to see anyone else getting hurt, or thought convincing Jed to leave town was a way to help Gemma.

Or…

"She might have known Jed would be murdered," he said.

"She couldn't have."

"Does she know anyone close to Grayson? Someone who would have known Jed would be killed?"

"Alan," Gemma breathed incredulously. "She said he worked at the community center, 'doing things for Samuel.' I couldn't believe she was interested in him. He looked like a gangster."

"'Doing things for Samuel'?" Ford nodded. Was he doing things for Samuel by way of his henchmen? "She might have heard them talking. Or Alan told her. He could have been close enough to know the plans." He might have been tasked with doing the killing, too.

He printed the email and then sent it to his personal account. After deleting every trace of the email from Michael's inbox, sent and deleted folders, he got up from the office chair, stuffing the note with the password and the email into his pocket. "Let's go."

If Lacy had warned Jed, maybe there was hope for her yet. On the other hand, if she was beginning to see the truth about Grayson and his cult, she could be stepping onto dangerous ground. If Grayson found out what she'd done, or suspected her in any way…

Through the back door, Ford took Gemma's hand. When hers tightened in his, he felt an instant response. How she managed to elicit so much heat with so little coaxing disconcerted him. Right now he had to stay alert.

Reaching the front of the house, he spotted a car parked

across the street that hadn't been there before. There were two men inside.

"That's Alan," Gemma said. "In the passenger seat."

The two men started to get out. They hadn't searched Michael's house yet, but apparently would now.

"Let's go another way." Ford took her around the back, staying hidden by trees and thick vegetation in the neighboring front yard. Sneaking down the block, they made it to Ford's Escalade.

He opened the passenger door. "Get in."

Closing the door behind her, he went around to the driver's side, hoping Lacy's email wouldn't be discovered. He'd deleted the files but they could still be extracted.

"I need to go talk to Lacy," Gemma said.

"I'll go with you. I need to talk to her, too."

"No, Ford. She won't talk with you around. She must know how Bo feels about you. Samuel, too."

"It's too risky. Samuel will start to question your loyalty now."

"Surely he expects me to try and prove my innocence. He just doesn't want the identity of the killer to be exposed. He's tasked Bo with ensuring that. If he sees that I'm still close to Lacy, he might leave me alone."

"Lacy warned Jed, remember."

"He doesn't know that."

Yet. "All right, but I'm going to be waiting nearby."

The next day, Gemma put on her best Devotee face and headed for Cold Plains Coffee. Ford waited in the Escalade, blue eyes hidden behind dark sunglasses, elbow on the open window frame. Sexy. Gorgeous. Armed and carrying his badge.

Pushing the door open, Gemma spotted Lacy and hoped she was right about her friend, that she'd warned Jed because she knew what kind of man Samuel really was. That she was turning her back on his cult. That way, Gemma could keep her friend.

Lacy beamed a brilliant, happy smile when she saw Gemma and Gemma smiled back. Was it genuine? Was Lacy truly her friend or did she have another reason for warning Jed? A more sinister one?

"Gemma." Lacy wove her way around workers and the counter, whisking past a short line of pinkies-up Cold Plains residents and gracefully wrapped her arm around Gemma. "I've been so worried about you."

"You heard, huh?"

Lacy let her go. "Who hasn't? Your bracelet was found at your ex's crime scene. It was in the paper."

"I didn't kill him."

"Of course you didn't, Gemma."

Was she being sarcastic? If so, she was making light of a serious situation, a situation that could affect the rest of Gemma's life. Gemma didn't appreciate that.

"Someone stole my bracelet. I'm being set up."

"Oh, nobody thinks you killed him anyway. You'll be fine, you wait and see."

Taken aback, Gemma wondered what had prompted Lacy to say that. How could she know what everybody thought? And who was 'everybody'?

"Where's Ford?" Lacy leaned around her to look through the front windows. "I heard he was living with you again."

Seeing that Lacy had spotted him outside in his SUV, Gemma didn't respond.

"Is he?" Lacy asked.

"For now." Gemma told her about the recording, watching her for signs of reaction. Lacy listened without a change in her demeanor.

"The forensics technician working on Jed's laptop was murdered and now the laptop is missing," Gemma said.

Lacy's mouth opened with her surprise. "Are you kidding?"

Was she sincere or had she known about Michael's murder? Gemma supposed it was possible she didn't. "I'll be charged with Jed's murder without that evidence."

Now Lacy batted her hand. "You don't have anything to worry about, Gemma. As long as you stay objective about Ford."

And there it was. Lacy did know something, even if it wasn't about the technician. "What do you mean?" What did Ford have to do with this?

"He's just been making a lot of waves lately."

"By helping me prove my innocence?" Unbelievable. Lacy was against Ford.

"You don't need him."

She sounded as though she were sure. "Why? Do you know who stole my bracelet?"

Lacy's lips twitched uncertainly, then she glanced around the coffee shop. Didn't she want anyone to hear?

"It's okay, you can tell me," Gemma said.

Lacy put her hand on Gemma's back and guided her toward the exit. "You shouldn't be here."

Abruptly, Gemma stopped and turned to face her. Lacy lowered her hand.

"I know about the email you sent Jed," Gemma said, quietly enough that no one would hear.

If that caught Lacy off guard, her friend did a great job of covering it. "Whatever are you talking about, Gemma?"

She was going to deny it? Who else would send the email? No one that Gemma knew. No one would take the risk. "I know you sent it."

"Gemma, if you would just leave well enough alone…"

"Well enough? Is being a suspect to murder 'well enough'?"

Lacy stared at Gemma for several seconds. "Ford…he's

staying with you and he's…" She couldn't seem to find the words.

"Helping me."

"He's causing trouble."

Gemma blinked in befuddlement a few times. "You encouraged me to be with him before. You said he was exactly the kind of cop this town needs."

"That was before I heard he went behind Bo's back."

"So now you're going to turn yours on me?"

Lacy sighed with exasperation. "What do you expect me to do?"

"Be my friend."

Lacy's lips pursed ever so slightly and her eyes wore an admonishing frown. "As long as you're with him, you're not one of us, Gemma."

"One of whom?" A Devotee?

"I like you, I really do. But I have to be careful now."

Lacy had to be careful with Gemma, because Gemma was with Ford, a cop who played by the rules. Rules that Bo and Samuel wanted to break. The sting of her friend's rejection pierced deep.

"If Ford is going rogue you could be in so much trouble, Gemma. You have no idea."

Her warning was clue enough. "Did Alan tell you about the computer?" He must have.

Lacy's head jerked backward as though she was suddenly aware of the slip. "No. You're all everyone is talking about right now, that's all."

"Rumors?" That was the best she could do? Lacy was lying.

"Yes. Of course. How else would I know?"

"Right. How else? Why don't you tell me that, Lacy? And while you're at it, why don't you tell me why you warned Jed that if he didn't leave town, he might be killed?"

Lacy's head jerked again, her nonchalance faltering once

more. "Gemma, you're talking nonsense. I have nothing to do with your dilemma."

"My dilemma?" This was getting more and more inconceivable by the second. Lacy was denying everything. Staying true to Samuel, even though her action in sending the email suggested otherwise. "What do you know about the computer?"

Lacy scoffed. "Oh, Gemma, stop. It's nothing."

Nothing. Gemma was being framed for murder and it was nothing. "You just told me I could be in trouble."

Lacy glanced around again.

"Afraid someone's going to hear you?"

Growing angry, Lacy locked her gaze with Gemma's.

Gemma didn't back down. "Is Alan one of Samuel's henchmen?"

Lacy's anger intensified. "Take my advice, Gemma. Get away from Ford. He's on his way down, but it's not too late for you."

"Is he?" And why was it not too late for her? Would Samuel look the other way if she became one of his followers? And would Samuel still feel the same if he discovered Gemma could be pregnant?

"He doesn't fit in here. He's against everything Samuel has built for this town."

"Listen to what you're saying. Do you really think the success of a town depends on one person? Samuel is over the top. He's crazy."

"I think it's time you left."

Was Lacy afraid or was she protecting her idyllic life by sidling under Samuel's wing? "Did Alan kill Jed?"

"Leave." Now Lacy pointed toward the doors.

"You're the first friend I met here, Lacy. I care about you. And I'm worried *you're* the one who's in trouble."

An eerie resignation seeped into Lacy's eyes. "I know there's no convincing you of the folly of staying with Ford, but I'm here to tell you that if you do—" her voice lowered to a whisper "—you'll be cast out from this town. Or worse." The last she all but hissed.

"Ford won't let that happen. And we aren't going anywhere."

"You're going to go up against Samuel?"

"If he's setting me up for murder, yes."

That eerie resignation deepened. "Then you and I can't be friends anymore."

Had Lacy chosen sides? She'd chosen Samuel? Heartache crushed Gemma. "If that's how you really feel…"

Lacy held a steady face, breaking Gemma's heart further. "Just go, Gemma."

"All right." Gemma turned, numb, and walked toward the door, suffocating beneath the stares of Cold Plains Coffee's rich patrons.

Stopping at the door, she looked back. Lacy's eyes narrowed and with a disgusted swat of her hand, she marched toward the back of the coffee shop.

Dismissed. As easy as that.

It didn't seem possible. What about the email? What about their friendship? Hadn't any of that meant anything?

Chapter 9

"Put yourself in her shoes, Gemma."

Gemma looked up at Ford from where she sulked on her living-room sofa.

"She's a Devotee. That means she's inside Grayson's most secretive circle. If she's discovered things about him that are incriminating, he'll kill her if she deviates at all."

"Then we have to help her."

He came to her and sat down, putting his arm around her. "We will, but it will have to be from a distance."

She snuggled closer to him.

"We can't put her in any danger."

"Is that why she sent me away like that? Was she protecting me?"

"And herself. Maybe. She may also be genuinely loyal to Grayson."

Gemma pulled back from Ford's comforting embrace. Why didn't he believe Lacy wasn't completely under Samuel's mind control? "She warned Jed he was about to be killed."

"She liked you. You were her friend. She must have known about the bracelet and that you'd be a suspect because of it. I can see how she'd be torn enough to act. But now that Jed is gone and I kept key evidence hidden from Bo, she's made her decision. You're not part of Grayson's cult. She is."

And now they couldn't be friends. As upset as that made her, she understood Ford's point. He was right. Lacy was in too deep to find her way out. She was where she believed she was safest.

Sadness welled up and immersed Gemma's heart. She would mourn the loss of a friendship that had meant so much to her. She'd also mourn the loss of Cold Plains, or her perception of it. All she had were her possessions, each one blissfully purchased. But even those didn't matter anymore. There was nothing left for her here. Nothing except Ford.

Eyeing him, she saw his care and patience.

"Let's leave, Ford. Let's go away from here." She didn't mean it to sound as if they'd go together and live happily ever after.

"I'm not leaving Cold Plains," he said, alleviating her concern and disappointing her at the same time. "I'm staying until Samuel Grayson is brought to justice."

She should have known he'd say that. He'd stay and see that his hometown was purged of crime, lawman that he was.

"And you're staying with me," he added.

Wishing he was saying that for a different reason, she broke her gaze from his. In the next instant, she wished she could turn off the switch that made her desire to be with him. Unfortunately there was none, and she couldn't stop the way she felt. And that would only get more difficult if she was pregnant.

Reaching for her, he touched her face, turning her head

toward him and bringing her gaze back to him. "Everything will be all right. I'll make sure of it."

What about them?

As they continued to fall into each other's eyes, she felt their increasingly familiar chemistry fire to life. Ford ran his thumb over her mouth.

"Don't look so sad, Gemma. I want to see your smile again."

"I want to see your badge again."

With a single, breathy laugh, he angled his head and kissed her. What he'd likely intended to be a casual response morphed into more. Immediate passion erupted. Gemma parted her lips to seek more of him and he pressed harder for a deeper kiss.

Sliding her arms around him as he leaned toward her, she lay back on the sofa. He climbed over her, giving her room to move her legs up and onto the sofa. She opened her knees and he fitted himself between them, coming down for another fervent kiss. Everywhere his body came in contact with hers, a burning fire blazed.

"Gemma," he rasped. "Gemma."

"Make love to me," she said.

He groaned as his cell phone once again interrupted. Ignoring it, he continued kissing her, heating her up until she felt flushed with need.

His cell phone rang for the third time.

Ford lifted his head and stared down at her.

She wanted him so badly. But his ringing phone had spared them from making another mistake.

He retrieved his phone and put it to his ear as he rose to stand.

"McCall." As he listened his face lost all traces of passion. "We're on our way."

He disconnected.

"Who was that?" she asked.

After a brief hesitation, he said. "Hawk Bledsoe. An FBI agent working with a task force to bring Grayson down. He may have found Felix Taylor."

"You're working with the FBI?"

"We need to meet him. Let's get going."

Gemma tried not to put too much importance on the fact that he'd told her who his secret friend was. He'd told her who Hawk Bledsoe was because he had to, but he hadn't admitted to working with him.

"How did you find out about a John Doe in a mountain town like Shady Meadow?" Hallie asked with a shaking voice.

Sandwiched between her distraught grandmother and Dillon in the back seat of Ford's Escalade, Hallie was tense, her emotions on the verge of erupting.

"I gave his picture and name to a friend of mine, who entered it into a database. When I met with him yesterday, he said he got a call from the sheriff there and gave me the specifics of the crime scene."

"Do you think it's my dad?"

Martha turned stark, reddened eyes toward him from her dreadful stare out the window.

"I don't know."

Either Hallie or her grandmother would have to identify the murder victim. Hallie realized that and exchanged a look with Martha.

"We'll be there with you," Gemma said, her heart breaking for them both.

"H-how did he die?" Tears brimmed her lower lids.

"We don't know for sure if it's your father," Ford reminded her.

"Just tell me."

Ford glanced at Gemma and then into the rearview mirror. Seconds later, he finally and slowly said, "He was hanged, but his body was found along the side of a highway." The rope had still been around his neck, Agent Bledsoe had said.

Gemma felt the raw emotion inside the vehicle.

"S-somebody dumped him there?" Her voice shook again.

"Yes."

Martha resumed her awful, silent stare through the window. She must know they'd find her son at the county morgue. Despondently, Hallie leaned on Dillon, who put his arm around her and pulled her closer.

Ford drove to a stop in front of the county coroner's office. Hallie walked with her grandmother and Dillon trailed behind as they all entered the small building.

After a receptionist phoned in their arrival, a medical examiner emerged from a hallway. Average in height and in an open white medical jacket, he stepped toward Ford, seeing his badge.

"Dr. Owens."

"Ford McCall." They shook hands. "This is Hallie and Martha Taylor."

The medical examiner regarded them with empathy. "I know this is difficult, so why don't we just get to it?"

Hallie nodded, sniffling and wiping her eyes.

The man led them down a gray, cold hallway. Gemma took Ford's hand and he gave it a squeeze. She didn't have a father, but facing identifying the body of anyone close to the heart had to be daunting.

The medical examiner pushed open a door and walked into a long, narrow room full of refrigerated coffin drawers. One was pulled out and a body covered in a white sheet lay there.

The medical examiner stood on the other side of the flat drawer. "Are you ready?"

Martha covered her mouth and began crying.

"Go ahead," Hallie said bravely. "Grandma, close your eyes."

Waiting a beat or two, the medical examiner pulled down the white sheet.

Martha burst into greater sobs.

"Yes," Hallie choked. "That's him. That's my dad." Then she buried her face against her grandmother and the two cried, holding each other.

Gemma wiped away her own tears rolling down her face. Damn that Samuel Grayson. He had to be stopped.

"He was hit on the head with a blunt object," the medical examiner said to Ford. "Probably before he was hanged."

Just like Jed and Michael, the technician.

Dillon moved to Hallie and her grandmother, putting his hand on Hallie's back and rubbing gently.

Hallie turned into his arms. "Bo Fargo can't get away with this."

"It's Samuel who's behind it, Hallie," Dillon said. "He's the one who did this."

Ford put his arm around Martha, who leaned against him and looked forlornly toward the drawer. The medical examiner had covered the body again.

"My son was murdered," Martha lamented. Then she looked up at Ford. "You have to do something."

"I'll catch the killer. You have my word."

Gemma felt his resolve ring true. Ford wouldn't give up until he found justice for all of Bo and Samuel's victims.

After driving Dillon, Martha and Hallie back to Cold Plains, Ford and Gemma returned to Shady Meadows. Ford wanted to check around town and ask a few questions. He was quiet all the way to their motel. Gemma wondered if he was thinking about Felix or if it bothered him to be alone with her again. She was stuck with him, and it was beginning to really weigh on her that she might be pregnant. Maybe she'd pick up a test. No point in upsetting him if it was a false alarm. She'd have to figure out how to get the test without him knowing, though.

She could just see him catching her standing in front of the pregnancy tests.

What are you doing? he'd ask.

To which she'd have no reply. Somehow, *Oh, I thought these were the tampons,* wouldn't fly.

Entering the motel room, he dropped the overnight bag they'd decided to share outside the bathroom.

"Are you hungry?"

She shook her head. Her nerves had wiped out all her hunger pains.

"Is something wrong?"

"No." She tried to sound cheery. *A-okay. Never better. Nothing wrong here. Nope.*

Oh, by the way, I think I'm pregnant.

He stood in the middle of the room, uncharacteristically awkward. He rubbed the back of his neck. Glanced at the door as if contemplating escaping for a little while. Gemma began to feel ill at ease.

"Is something wrong with you?"

Dropping his hand, he turned his head toward her. "Me? No. I just notice how sometimes you seem…upset about something."

Crap. "Me?"

"Yeah."

"Then stop acting like it's killing you to be in the same room with me."

He stared at her. "It is."

That threatened to send her into a meltdown. It was killing him because he wanted her. "Then do something about it." She wished she could take the words back as soon as she said them. She couldn't think clearly when he was around.

"Trust me, I'd like to."

She may as well forge ahead. "What's stopping you?"

"If we continue like this, we might not be able to walk away from it."

A sharp stab of despondency slammed her. He would walk away? "Don't you mean *you* won't be able to walk away?"

He sighed a heavy breath and ran his fingers through his thick, blond hair, confirmation enough for her.

"Why would you walk away?" He was that sure?

"It's not you, it's…"

His family. His wife. His unborn baby. "Are you that afraid of losing another person you love?" That had to be the crux of his emotional trouble.

"I'm not afraid, I just…I can't be involved with anyone right now."

"How will you know when you can?"

"What are you asking? Are you ready for another relationship?"

She lowered her head. She'd always told herself that she needed to heal from Jed's destruction before she gave love a try again. Before she could learn to trust a man again. Had Jed's murder and all the trouble Samuel caused diverted her from that goal? She'd no longer have the seminars to help her. She couldn't possibly be ready, and yet… She lifted her head.

"Now you see my point."

He was turning this all back onto her. "Ford, you haven't let go of your guilt over not being able to save your family." And then his wife had died during childbirth. Had he ever known love without losing it to tragedy?

"I have let go. I spend every day of my life atoning for that. Avenging them. I do what I do for them. Not because I feel guilty."

"And your wife? What about her death?" She didn't have to add that he'd lost his unborn son as well.

He pointed his finger at her. "Don't."

His family's murders and the death of his wife and son had marred him irrevocably. "I'm not going to die, Ford."

"It's not that."

"Isn't it?"

He stared his warning.

"You're afraid of falling in love."

"I'm not afraid," he snapped.

He was. He was terrified. He couldn't bear to lose another person he loved. So he guarded himself against it. He made sure he didn't feel enough to make it impossible to walk away. As long as he knew he could walk away, he felt safe. He might tell himself that some day, when he was ready, he'd try love again. But he'd never be ready unless he faced his fear.

What would it do to him if she was pregnant?

Gemma trotted to keep up with Ford's long, angry strides. He was still mad at her for pinning him with a hurtful truth last night. Well, that truth hurt her, too. He still denied that his wife's and baby's deaths kept him shying away from love. The big, strong, tough cop couldn't possibly be afraid of something as harmless as love. But he was.

They'd spent the night in separate beds. She'd lain awake tortured by his closeness, wondering how he separated not wanting to lose another person he loved with fear of love. Maybe he felt that as long as it was his cognitive decision, it wasn't fear.

She followed him up the steps of an old, rundown cabin. The sheriff had said Felix's body had been found just outside of town, not far from the road leading here. This was the only house within reasonable distance.

Ford knocked. No one answered. "There's no one there."

Gemma turned with Ford. A boy riding a mountain bike and dressed in khaki shorts and a green T-shirt had stopped in the driveway, his curly red hair springing out from under a baseball cap.

"You lost?" the boy asked.

"Do you live near here?" Ford countered non-committally.

"Yeah, over that mountain there." He pointed. "On a ranch."

"Do you know the people who live here in this cabin?"

"There's just one. A man. A real loner. My mom says she feels sorry for him because he doesn't have any family. He only comes here for the summer. Has a house in Florida. Must've decided to stay there this year. Nobody's seen him. How come you're here?"

"A man was murdered recently and we wanted to ask him if he saw anything."

"Oh, yeah, I heard about that. He was dumped just at the end of this driveway." The boy pointed there. "Do you think he did it?"

"We don't know yet. Thanks for your help."

"See ya around." The boy peddled off, glancing back at them once, his bike zigzagging as he picked up speed down the driveway, veering off at a trail.

"So much for asking the neighbors," Gemma said.

Ford began walking around the cabin, stopping at a window to peer in. Drapes blocked his view. He continued along the side and peered in another window. Something must have caught his eye because he returned to the front door.

"Back up, Gemma."

She did. "What are you going to do?"

Her answer came when he lifted his leg and kicked, breaking the wood holding the door shut. It swung open and Gemma was immediately accosted by a horrible stench.

Gagging, she covered her mouth and nose. Around Ford's big frame, she saw a man hanging from a rope. A badly decomposed man. His clothes hung, dirty and stained, on rotting flesh.

She screamed.

Ford stepped inside, already reaching for his cell phone. He hadn't bothered with his gun. The man had obviously been dead a long time. Shaking, she watched him go to the chair near the body and look down at a baseball bat. Jed's killer had used one on him. And in all likelihood, Felix, too. That and the proximity to Felix's body suggested this man had seen something that had cost him his life. The sheriff had probably knocked and when no one answered, assumed the man was still in Florida.

Gemma watched Ford search around the house, unable to look as he went through the man's clothing. Nothing else must have turned up because he ushered her out of the house empty-handed.

"Why does the killer leave baseball bats at the scene?" she asked.

"Must be his method. He knocks his victims out and then hangs them. Catches them unaware so there's no struggle. No noise. Killing them is easy. He's careful not to leave any prints or other evidence. Only the ropes and the bats."

"But he doesn't leave a bat at every scene."

"No. Which tells me he didn't want Felix to be connected to the other murders. Jed and Michael, he wanted connected."

"In case he had to pin me with both?"

"Could be. Leaving the weapon is ballsy, though."

"He must not be afraid of being caught."

"No. But that could work in our favor."

Because the killer was overconfident. Because he had Samuel backing him, or so he believed. Gemma shuddered. She wished all this would end. She'd moved to Cold Plains to find peace, not to encounter one dead body after another.

"Come on," Ford said. "The sheriff is on the way. I don't want to be here too long."

As he drove down the driveway and onto the highway, she recognized a car parked along the side of the road. The same one that had been outside the forensic scientist's house. And inside the car were Alan and the same driver as before.

Ford cursed. He hadn't wanted Samuel to learn what he'd discovered. "Let's get our things and drive back to your place tonight."

Gemma was in complete agreement. She'd get no sleep whatsoever knowing they were being watched. But would they be any less watched back in Cold Plains?

Chapter 10

Dillon's dad was hell bent on going to the community center again tonight. Dillon reclined on the family-room sectional, tossing a football up into the air and catching it. He was waiting for Hallie. She was coming over tonight. His parents were in the kitchen on the other side of the wall. His Mom hadn't been drinking and was thinking clearly again. So far the argument was benign, but he could hear the tension building in his dad.

He hadn't told his parents he'd gone to Shady Meadow to identify Hallie's dad. He didn't trust his own dad.

"You're going, and you'll act like a wife is supposed to act," his dad yelled. He hadn't yelled until now.

"That would be fine if I had a husband who acted the way a husband was supposed to act!"

Curtis swore viciously.

Catching the football again, Dillon put it on the couch next to him and jumped to his feet.

"You can't boss me around anymore, Curtis. I'm not going

to any more seminars. I'm also not going to any event where that repulsive Samuel Grayson will be!"

"I'm sick of your back talk. You'll do what I tell you to do from now on, you hear me?"

Dillon entered the kitchen just as his dad slugged his mom. Her head jerked back and to the side with the impact and she cried out in pain.

Furious, Dillon stormed between them, slapping his hand on his dad's chest and shoving hard. His dad stumbled backward, startled. Dillon swung his fist and smashed his dad in the eye. Curtis grunted and stumbled again. He was a big man. It would take a lot to knock him down.

"Touch her again and you'll get more of that."

His dad was so stunned he didn't say anything.

"Mom isn't going to go to those stupid seminars anymore."

As he recovered from the surprise of his son's punch, Curtis's anger diminished. He turned to Dillon's mom. "Honey? You know I only want what's best for you. Sometimes that means you should do what I tell you."

With her hand on her cheek, his mom only looked at him incredulously.

"What's best for her is for you to keep your hands off her," Dillon said.

"Stay out of this, Dillon. Your mother and I have a life here that I'm trying to preserve."

"No, *you* have a life here," his mom said. "My life is going to be somewhere else." She dropped her hand from her cheek. "I want a divorce."

Pride and satisfaction and love expanded in Dillon.

"You've abused me for the last time," she added. "And so has Samuel."

"Samuel wouldn't hurt you. You don't understand. He's a positive influence on everyone."

"He's only looking out for *himself.* You're just too brainwashed to see it."

"No, you don't understand."

She turned for the stairs. "I'm going to pack a few things now and I'll be back for the rest later." She paused on the stairs. "Dillon, where have you been staying?"

"At Martha and Hallie Taylor's. There's plenty of room for you there. I'll call them."

"I won't impose. Maybe we should find another place, at least until the divorce is final."

"Don't worry about a place to stay. There are no Samuel sympathizers at Hallie's. They'll welcome you with open arms." He looked pointedly at his dad, who was beginning to seem broken. Desperate.

He'd have to watch him. And his mom. He'd make sure she was safe.

"You're tearing this family apart," Curtis told his son.

Dillon went to stand at the bottom of the stairs, blocking his dad's path in case he decided to follow his mom. "You hit her."

"You don't know what you're doing. We were a perfect family."

"Is that what all your friends over at the community center think? Do they know how many times you beat your wife?"

"Your mom and I have some problems, but we can work them out."

By following Samuel? "Don't even try to go near her again." Hearing his mom emerge from the master bedroom, he leaned closer to his dad. "Hit her again, I'll hurt you worse than you ever hurt her."

"I'm your father." He was only worried about appearances. Inside, he was an angry man who needed a punching bag. Well, his mother was no longer going to serve that purpose. From now on, his dad had to make his own way. Without her.

Dillon wondered how long it would take for Samuel to catch on to the imperfection.

His dad must have been wondering the same thing. As

soon as his mother reached the bottom stair, his dad lunged for her, yelling, "I won't let you destroy me!"

Ford put to good use the overpriced spices and tuna steaks Gemma had gotten from the health food market in town. Only the best could be bought there, and she had relished the hundreds she'd spent. It wasn't his cooking that had her riveted, though. He was still in uniform and that was playing havoc on her senses. Even with Bo so out of favor with him, he hadn't stopped going to work.

He stirred the brown sauce simmering on the stove, but it was his hand that she admired. His strong hand that could be so gentle with her.

Lifting a spoonful of the brown sauce to her mouth, he looked into her eyes as she tasted the concoction. It could have been vinegar and she wouldn't have noticed. She loved how his eyes reached into her, tickling her soul.

"Mmm." The murmur was for him, not the sauce.

His deep chuckle communicated mutual warmth. She could stare at him for hours, giddy with the way he made her feel.

She slid her hand up his chest, over his badge where her fingers traced the outline. Some day she was going to have to wear that thing. Maybe she'd put it around her neck with nothing else on...

"Stop that."

"Stop what?" She moved her hand to his stubbly face, loving the manly texture. There was no stopping any of this. Him. Her. This crazy passion they had.

His head dipped. Looping her arm around his neck, she tipped hers up and his mouth brushed hers. She felt his warm breath, stared into his blue eyes, melting.

And then a knock on the door jerked them apart. He seemed too glad for the interruption, then his gaze turned hard with disgruntlement. He didn't like his lack of control.

He went to the door and opened it to Bo Fargo. What was he doing here?

"Sorry to bother you so late," Bo said, bowing his head to Gemma. To Ford he said, "I need a word with you."

Ford stepped aside and Bo entered.

Gemma moved to stand next to Ford and Bo stayed in the entryway.

"Would you like to sit down?" Gemma asked. "Can I get you anything?"

"No, ma'am. This won't take long. Ford, I heard you took the Taylors to Shady Meadow and identified Felix Taylor's body."

"How did you hear that?" Gemma asked. The man sure had gall. They all knew he'd sent Alan to follow them.

"It just so happens that Lacy's boyfriend went to visit a friend there and saw you."

It just so happens...

"I planned to close out the Missing Persons report on him tomorrow," Ford said.

"Ford, I asked you to tell me about your activities, and that includes your interactions with Dillon Monroe."

"Felix was Martha Taylor's son."

"Yes, but her granddaughter has been cavorting with Dillon. They've been stalking Samuel, stirring up trouble, as you well know. We need to keep close tabs on them."

Stalking Samuel? Stirring up trouble?

"Hallie was trying to find her father, and Dillon is worried about his mother," Gemma said. "How does that qualify as trouble?"

"They should leave that to the law," Bo answered, affronted.

"They did," Gemma argued with a note of deliberate innocence. "They let Ford handle everything."

Bo's look hardened but he kept his tone patient. "I stopped by to ask you again, Ford, to keep me informed of your activities, particularly when they involve the Monroes. I've asked you before. Don't make me ask you again."

"I'll do my best, Chief."

Gemma wondered if Bo saw the twinkle of mischief in Ford's eyes. He gave no indication that he had as he bade them farewell and left.

"I should let you handle him more often," Ford said with a grin.

"He sure was nice."

"That's because there isn't a damn thing he can do about it."

But that hadn't stopped him from trying to control Ford.

His cell phone rang.

"McCall."

Gemma could hear the frantic voice of a woman shouting.

"Calm down, Hallie. Where are you?"

"At Dillon's!" Gemma heard her yell, followed by more frantic shouting.

"We're on our way. Don't go inside. Wait in your car, okay?"

Hallie must have answered agreeably in a lower tone. Ford tucked his phone away.

"Dillon and his dad got into a fight and his mother tried to stop them. Curtis started beating her."

"Oh, my God. What's Hallie doing there?"

"She was meeting Dillon there because they had plans to go to the community center to keep an eye on his mom. She heard fighting when she reached the door and didn't go in."

Gemma hurried out the door with him. "Are you going to call Bo?"

"Hell, no."

She loved his unwavering boldness. Hopping into his SUV, they raced across town.

When Ford screeched to a halt at an angle in front of the Monroe home, Hallie emerged from her car. Hearing elevated voices from inside the house, Gemma knew the fight wasn't over. She and Hallie followed Ford.

He stopped and turned. "You both wait here."

Then he drew his gun and went up the stairs. Opening the door, he raised his weapon and disappeared inside. Gemma exchanged a look with Hallie and in unison they both started toward the house.

"Stay behind me," Gemma told Hallie.

She peered inside the open door. Ford was already cuffing Curtis on the kitchen floor. His face was bloody. Dillon stood next to his crying mother, his face also bloody from their fistfight. Gemma spotted bruises on Mrs. Monroe's face and arms.

Ford helped Curtis to his feet. "Dillon, you take your mother to the hospital." Then he looked at Gemma. "You come with me."

He was sure sexy when he was in charge. She followed him as he pushed Curtis, who was craning his neck to look over his shoulder, toward the door.

"Remember what I told you," Curtis warned his wife.

"Be quiet." Ford jerked him forward again.

"You better listen to me!" Curtis yelled.

Dillon put his arm around his mother and walked to the door. "Don't listen to him. He can't hurt you if he's in jail."

Gemma saw the way his mother cowered at Curtis's warning and wondered if she'd go through with her statement against her husband.

Early the next morning, Ford's cell phone rang again. Rolling toward the nightstand in Gemma's guest room, he checked the digital clock. Really early—4:00 a.m. early.

What now? "McCall."

"It's Dillon. Bo let my dad out last night. He said there wasn't enough evidence to charge him."

He swung his legs over the bed. "What?" He stood up.

"Bo came to see Mom at the hospital. To get her statement, he claimed. He said there probably wasn't enough evidence against my dad to hold him and told her to *think carefully* about what had happened. She said she fell down the stairs."

Damn. His mother was afraid to press charges. "Where are you now? Where is your mother?"

"We're back at the hospital. My mom went home after she was treated the first time. We were going to meet at Hallie's after she went home to get more things. I didn't think my dad would be released so soon. He beat her bad."

And now she was in the hospital, this time with more serious injuries. Ford cursed vehemently. "That son of a...!" Holding the phone between his shoulder and ear, he yanked on his jeans.

"I should have gone with her."

Hearing the catch in Dillon's voice, Ford said, "You didn't know. Is she going to be okay?"

"Yeah. They want to keep her today to monitor her head injuries. My dad used a bat on her. I hid it in the garage behind the trash cans."

A bat...

Ford praised Dillon's quick thinking while the significance of the bat sank in. Was Curtis responsible for the other murders? If so, he'd made a mistake using a bat on his wife. He'd beat his wife with a bat! Such a tide of rage filled Ford he wasn't sure he could contain it. This would not have happened had Curtis been kept in jail.

"I'll be there as soon as I can."

His hands trembled as he disconnected. Putting on a shirt, he climbed the stairs to wake Gemma.

Feeling Gemma glance over at him every few minutes, Ford tried to maintain a normal appearance of calm, while inside, fury burned. Bo tried to thwart him at every turn, and this time he'd succeeded. His blatant disregard for the law was taking its toll. He had to be patient, wait until the FBI had enough on Samuel's cult to arrest everyone involved. But the injustice reminded too much of what he'd lost.

He stopped in front of the Monroes' house.

"What are you going to do?" Gemma inquired.

Without responding, he picked up his cell phone and called a detective he thought he could trust. After instructing the man to come to this address prepared to process a crime scene, he disconnected.

"Wait here." He got out of the SUV and shut the door.

Gemma got out, too. "Ford…"

"I'm going to keep Bo from preventing another arrest," he said. "The detective won't be here for a few minutes. That gives me time to gather my own evidence." Just in case.

Her eyes softened with understanding. Going up on her toes, she gave him a quick peck of a kiss. "Be careful."

Did she trust him not to cross a line? She must. He had his doubts, but she trusted him, had faith in his ethics as a cop. She'd suffered at the hands of a wife-beater. She had no sympathy for men like Curtis, but preferred the way of the law. That struck a chord in him, connected them even more than they already were. Not analyzing it too much, he strode up the walkway to the front door. He rang the bell several times.

The door opened and Curtis appeared, standing in a robe. Seeing Ford, he demanded belligerently, "What are you doing back here?"

The man had beaten his wife. Put her in the hospital. And now he felt untouchable. With Samuel and the Chief of Police behind him, he had good reason. There was nothing Ford could do. Or so Curtis thought…

"May I come in?" Ford asked.

Curtis stepped aside. "Sure." He was cocky with self-confidence, but Ford detected a note of uncertainty.

Wanting to punch the man until he begged him to stop,

beat him until he cried out in pain, until he had to be taken to the hospital just like his wife, Ford steered his course straight. A police officer didn't do things like that. Police officers upheld the law, they didn't break the law. His inability to uphold the law the first time he'd been here made him furious. There was no justice when a criminal got away with his crime. It left victims helpless. And Ford knew all too well what that felt like.

Suddenly he was back in time, a fourteen-year-old waking to the sound of crashing furniture and the pleas of his father. Gunshots. Screams. He'd gotten out of bed and gone into the hallway. One of the gunmen had just passed his room. The screams were concentrated in his parents' bedroom.

Ford had waited in his room, scared and not knowing what to do. He had no phone and the closest one was downstairs. When he peered through the crack of his door, he saw his little brother run down the hall. A gunman chased him down the stairs. Ford followed slowly. But once he'd reached the lower level, he'd ducked into the stairwell to the basement. He'd shut the door behind him. Waiting there, rigid with fear, he'd heard the gunshot that had killed his little brother. His mother was screaming. Alone and crying, he'd listened to the two robbers ransack the house. The last of the screams from his mother had faded. When he'd heard footsteps approach the basement door, he'd run downstairs and hidden.

Long minutes passed before the robbers left and he'd emerged from the basement to find his family dead. He'd learned later that his mother had been raped before she was killed. The sound of her screams haunted him to this day.

Seeing Curtis eyeing him with mocking impatience, Ford put the memories back where they belonged, away from his heart and in a dark hole that fueled his passion for justice.

"Where's your wife?" he asked.

Curtis hesitated and Ford could see him scramble for a lie. "I don't know. She wasn't here when I got home."

Seeing three deep scratch marks on his cheek that hadn't been there before, Ford grabbed Curtis's chin and angled his face to see them better. "Where'd you get those?"

"I tripped coming out of the community center."

"After hours?"

"Samuel sometimes has…parties."

The man was a really bad liar. "Mind if I have a look around?"

Curtis shrugged, theatrically overconfident. Foolish. "Sure."

Ford walked farther into the living room. Nothing was out of place, but it looked freshly cleaned. He saw an area on the carpet that appeared to have been scrubbed. Bending over, he felt the carpet. It was damp and he could see the remnants of bloodstains. Removing the camera he'd brought with him, he began snapping pictures.

"What are you doing?" Curtis asked.

"Routine."

"You didn't take pictures before."

A baseball bat wasn't part of the equation then. Not responding, Ford checked the kitchen and two bedrooms downstairs before heading upstairs.

In the master bedroom, there was an open suitcase on one side of the bed. It was partially filled with clothing. Curtis had caught his wife in the middle of packing, the catalyst to the fight. The use of a bat definitely revealed the man's passion. He took more pictures.

Back downstairs, he went into the garage and found the bat right where Dillon had directed him. He took pictures, leaning over the garbage cans to get close-ups of the blood drying on the end.

"Hey. What are you doing out here?" Curtis looked down at what he could see of the bat and his gaze swung back to Ford.

He hadn't been able to find it before now.

"I'm placing you under arrest for assault." Ford read Curtis Monroe his rights as he pulled out some handcuffs. "Turn around."

Curtis's round eyes regained their aura of false self-confidence. "You can't arrest me."

"I can and I will. Turn around."

Curtis raised his fist. Ford blocked it and pushed him back before he could make impact, sending him tripping over the step leading into the house. He bumped against the open door frame, pushed off that and lunged for Ford again.

Ford slammed his fist at the spot where Curtis's wife had scratched him in an attempt to defend herself. Curtis yelped as he landed on his hip on the step.

"If you want a room next to your wife at the hospital, I can arrange that," Ford cautioned, almost hoping the man would stand up and fight so he could follow through with his word.

Glaring from Ford's clenched fists to his face, Curtis didn't move, backing down.

"Stand up and turn around," Ford ordered.

He complied and Ford cuffed him. "Now sit down and wait."

Outside, Ford heard a car pull up and the engine die. Slipping on latex gloves, he pressed the garage-door button.

"What are you doing?"

Ignoring Monroe, Ford waited for the detective to appear.

"What have we got here?" the detective asked.

Ford explained everything Dillon had told him. "I'll take Mr. Monroe in, along with the weapon. I'll report the chain of custody and take care of the processing."

"The crime-scene team can handle that."

"I'll take care of the bat." He held up his camera. "I got pictures but you may want to get your own."

The detective stared at him for a long moment as the clear indication of distrust registered. "I understand, Deputy. Has anything been moved?"

"No. I waited for you."

Bo wouldn't be able to say they didn't have enough to hold Curtis. He was facing a felony that could carry as much as a twenty-year sentence, and there was nothing either Bo or Samuel could do about it.

Late night at the Cold Plains Police Department, Gemma walked proudly beside Ford down the long hallway adorned with pictures of Cold Plains. She hadn't stopped lusting over him since he'd got the call from Dillon. He was all grit and brawn, purpose and conviction. Her man.

She couldn't wait to be alone with him.

Just before they reached the door leading to the lobby, it opened and Bo appeared. Gemma stopped with Ford.

"In my office. Now." Bo passed them and turned a corner.

"I knew he wouldn't be happy," Ford mumbled.

"Is he going to fire you?"

"I don't care if he does."

He'd grown tired of working for a corrupt boss, such a complete opposite to himself, and Gemma sensed his resignation.

Bo led them into his office. Behind his desk, he leaned over and planted his hands on it. "I don't even know what to say to you."

"Upset that I arrested Curtis again?"

"Don't mock me, McCall. You're on a thin sheet of ice right now."

"I arrested Curtis for beating his wife with a baseball bat. Is that what you asked me in here to talk about?"

"I asked you in here to find out why you didn't call me."

"I wanted the charges to stick this time."

Gemma had no doubt Ford's sureness had found its mark. A flicker of anger crossed Bo's eyes and his mouth twitched. "I'm not sure I understand. Why don't you explain why you acted on your own?"

"I didn't. Dillon called me directly. Turns out his dad was released from jail and went home to find his wife packing to leave him. That made him pick up a baseball bat and beat her so badly that she's now in the hospital. I called Detective Adams and waited for him to arrive at the scene before I took control of the chain of custody on the weapon. I turned the bat over to evidence, and forensics is running a test on some blood found at the scene. All I need now is a statement from Mrs. Monroe, but even without it, I have enough to lock Curtis up for a long time."

"I told you to call me if anything else happened with the Monroes."

"And I ignored you."

Gemma cheered on the inside.

Bo trembled with barely contained rage. There was little the chief could say or do. He couldn't stop Ford from sending Curtis to jail.

"Samuel should be happy I'm clearing the town of another violent man," Ford said calmly. "It supports his idea of a perfect town. Or is there something special about Curtis Monroe that I don't know?"

All traces of menace vanished in Bo, expertly managed by a ruthlessly calculating man. Practiced professionalism. All an act.

"You're right, McCall. Aside from not following my orders, you did everything right. Samuel will be happy."

Straightening, Bo moved around the desk and came to stand in front of Ford and Gemma. "But keep in mind that I can fire you for not following my orders."

"I'm anxious to see what forensics comes up with on the bat." Ford wasn't fazed by Bo's intimidation.

"What's so special about the bat?"

"A bat was used on Jed and on the man found in Shady Meadow."

Gemma watched Bo digest that. Did Samuel's precious

Devotee like to leave breadcrumbs at his crime scenes? Had he killed Jed and the man from Shady Meadow?

Bo scoffed. "Curtis is hardly capable of killing anyone."

"But he's capable of bashing his wife's head in with a bat?"

"We're finished with this conversation. I came here tonight to give you a warning. It's the last one you'll get."

"Right. To follow your orders."

"Precisely."

"No warning necessary, Chief. I know exactly where I stand with you and Samuel."

Bo regarded him with reproach before turning to Gemma. "And where do you stand now?"

What was he asking?

"Samuel believes in your innocence, but I'm not sure he should," he said in her silence. "I'd sure hate to see that trust destroyed."

"With all due respect, Mr. Fargo, I don't see why my relationship with Samuel is any of your concern."

A half smile cocked Bo's mouth. "I just told you. He believes in your innocence."

"That's good. I am innocent."

"Unfortunately for you, I'm not as convinced. I received information just this afternoon that may change even Samuel's mind. It's regarding your ex-husband's estate. His attorney should be contacting you, maybe he already has tried." He glanced derisively at Ford. "But you haven't been available." Bo's gaze shifted back to her. "It seems Jed Johnson never changed his will after the two of you were divorced. He still has you named as his sole beneficiary. You inherit everything, Gemma. And it's a sizable estate."

She was rendered numb with whirling questions. How had he learned that, and was he threatening her?

"Jed?" she breathed incredulously.

He'd left her everything? If her bank account was burgeoning before, it was overflowing now. Had that been intentional or a mistake? He'd intended to bring her back home, maybe that was why in his warped thinking he'd left the will alone. Or he'd just been so crazed with the divorce that he'd let it slip she'd go with the latter. His money was too important to him. It had to be a mistake.

"Yes, Gemma, you're a very wealthy woman...if we can prove you didn't kill him."

He *was* threatening her. He was insinuating that she might have had a motive to murder her ex-husband. But if she stayed away from Ford, what then? Would he magically come up with proof of her innocence?

"If we're finished?" Ford interrupted.

"Think about what I've said, Gemma."

Ford guided Gemma out of the office. She still reeled with Bo's dangerous warning. By the time they left the building, fear overwhelmed her.

"What if he arrests me?"

"I'll prove you're innocent."

"What if you can't?"

"I will."

She admired his confidence. She wished she shared it. The recording was gone. There was nothing to exonerate her, and Bo might have plans to go through with his threat.

Chapter 11

After folding towels and putting them into the linen closet, Gemma stopped at the top of the stairs and listened. She didn't hear Ford. Living with him was a grueling exercise in self-control. After seeing him in action last night, she'd avoided him today as best she could. Her house wasn't enormous, though, and they'd had their run-ins. Coming out of the bathroom. In the kitchen for lunch. Hearing him moving about was equally tortuous. Closing the front door when he went on one of his patrols. Sliding the back door shut. The creak of the floor as he walked. The sound of him in the guest room.

How much more could she take? On top of the sizzling temptation of having a man who knew how to treat a lady in her house, there was too much jumbled up her mind. Jed. The whole mess with Samuel. Her possible pregnancy. All of it only added to the strain of chaining back her desire for Ford.

She was weary of it all. So was Ford. She could feel his tension, too.

He appeared at the bottom of the stairs.

"It's safe to come down," he said.

And she smiled hugely because he must think she was afraid, but not of him. Her smile took hold of him and what she saw triggered an answering response in her.

She stepped down the stairs and decided to let him think it wasn't him she wanted to avoid. "No sign of Bo or anyone else?"

"No."

"What do you think he'll do?"

"Wait for your next move." His eyes roamed her face, lingering on her eyes and mouth. Then he stepped back and turned, going to the sofa, where he sat.

Gemma sat next to him, curling her legs and rolling onto her hip. Her shoulder touched his arm and she would have moved over if he hadn't stretched his arm along the back of the sofa.

"He must know I won't join Samuel," she said, trying to sound normal. Inside, her heart sputtered with the thrill of his nearness.

"He might, but does Samuel?"

Samuel wanted her money. He had hopes that it wasn't too late to persuade her to come over to his side, to become a Devotee. She was an ideal candidate. Wealthy, healthy, young and attractive.

"Bo might convince him."

"Let him."

Hearing his frustration, she recalled Bo's warning. "What will you do if he fires you?"

After a moment of thought, he turned his head toward her. "For a long time I thought the only thing I wanted was to be a cop. Eventually to run the police department. It felt like my calling."

Because of what had happened to his family. "But now?"

"Now I'm not so sure. Sometimes I think I could do more good outside the police department."

"Do you mean independently?"

"Like private investigations."

Because of what Samuel was doing to the police department? It made sense. It also sounded as though he'd grown since he'd first become a cop. "Maybe it's time you stopped avenging your family. Maybe you've avenged them enough."

"You're going to bring that up again?"

Didn't he see that she had to? Maybe if she told him she thought she was pregnant…

"You'll always do what's right, Ford. Nothing or no one can take that away from you. Whether you're a cop or not, it doesn't matter. You're a good man. And it wasn't your fault that your family was killed."

"Stop, Gemma."

She couldn't. This was only part of what haunted him. And she needed to know if there was any chance for them. She would have preferred time alone, not to get involved so soon after her divorce, but if what they had was the rare and real thing, she wouldn't give up on him, especially not if she was pregnant.

"Let it go." She brushed her fingers along the back of his ear, feeling the strands of his blond hair. "Forgive yourself for being a fourteen-year-old who survived."

"You want me to forget?"

"No. Accept the fact that you had no control over what happened. You couldn't have stopped them from killing your parents and your brother. If you'd tried, you'd have been killed, too."

"Maybe."

"Would your mother have wanted you to try?"

She saw the answer in the grief that came into his eyes.

"No. She would have wanted you to live. So would your father and your brother."

Losing his family had driven him to become a cop and maybe there had been a time when he'd done it out of guilt, but she could tell he had different reasons now. Reasons that stemmed from a horrible tragedy that he'd turned into something good. Ford represented and stood for that good and he didn't back down in the face of evil. That's what made her love him.

Love…

Where had that word come from? Apprehension reared up in her. There was deeper pain in him than what had made him a cop. And it was that pain that would keep them apart, if he let it.

She began to move away from him. Maybe it would be better just to walk away, not to hope for a future.

He stopped her with his arm around her shoulder.

"You're right, Gemma."

She eased back against the sofa again, sinking into his blue eyes.

"I didn't realize until now, but I've made peace with that. I'm a cop so that I can stop crimes. That will never leave me. I don't do it to avenge anyone. Not anymore."

"What about your wife?" She asked quietly, not sure if she was ready to hear his answer.

It came in the hard barrier that shuttered his eyes. "She was something different."

Yes. Different. Damaging.

"Do you ever see yourself getting married again?" she gently asked, half of her wishing he wouldn't answer. That way she still had denial. Except she couldn't deny anymore.

"Maybe. Not for a while, though."

"How long?"

"I don't know. Ten, fifteen years from now."

"That's a long time from now."

"Yeah. Good."

Good? He wanted that much time to pass? Had he loved his wife that much? Had she been his true love and he didn't need to have another in this life? Was his job in law enforcement enough? He did pour himself into his work, all that goodness driving him.

Crushing disappointment made her withdraw. She moved away from him, leaning back but not getting up off the sofa.

Even if they decided to keep seeing each other, he wouldn't be there for her. Jed hadn't, either, in a different way, but he still hadn't been there for her. She couldn't do that again. She couldn't let herself down like that. The next time she gave her heart to a man, she'd know he felt the same.

Add onto that the possibility that she was pregnant and things got really complicated.

Disturbed, now Gemma did get up off the sofa, unfolding her legs and standing. She rubbed her arms and moved to the edge of the living room.

Ford came up behind her, putting his hands over hers and stilling them. "What's wrong, Gemma?"

She moved away from his touch and faced him. "Nothing."

"You've been acting strange lately."

"No, I haven't." She answered too quickly. "I haven't."

He scrutinized her in his cop way. "What's wrong, then?"

"Nothing. I just…I don't like hearing you say things like that." That wasn't completely true. She actually thought it was good he didn't want to settle down any time soon. She didn't, either. Well, not right away, anyway. Ten to fifteen years was too long for her, but two years seemed reasonable.

Running his hand through his thick blond hair, something she wished she had the liberty to do whenever the urge took her, he sighed and then looked at her in frustration. "I'm not planning anything, okay?"

His lack of resolve on the matter was palpable. He'd

thought about this and he'd thought about it long and hard. He didn't see himself married. And she couldn't be more convinced of his fear.

"We shouldn't even be having this conversation. I just got divorced from a monster. The last thing I need is another man."

There he went again, scrutinizing her. "Then why are we?"

What could she say? *I might be pregnant, that's why.* They could both be forced into a serious relationship before either of them was ready.

"I didn't see myself having sex with the cop who questioned me about my violent ex-husband."

His close scrutiny eased. "I didn't, either."

They shared a long look filled with knowing intimacy. Neither of them could deny the sex was good between them. That's why they hadn't been able to resist each other. She was also sure that's why neither of them had thought about birth control, not in the heat of the moment.

"Was it like that with your wife?" The question popped out. She hadn't intended to verbalize her curiosity. "I'm sorry, I shouldn't have asked that."

"No. It wasn't the way it is with you."

That he answered surprised her. He hadn't had with his wife what he had with Gemma. Did it mean anything more than sex?

Treading carefully, she asked, "How did you meet her?"

"We both went to the same college. I met her in a coffee shop. A year later she got pregnant and we married."

Gemma hid the flash of alarm that rushed to her nerve endings.

"After she died, I came back here," he continued. "It's the only place that's ever felt like home."

"I know what you mean."

"We do have that in common, don't we? Cold Plains." He grunted a cynical laugh.

They'd both come here seeking peace and ended up having to fight for it. She'd come to escape her ex-husband and he'd come to escape the darkness of his wife's death, to his hometown, where his family had lived, where his memories were, both good and bad. In the short time she'd been here, it had become that to her, too. Something bad had brought them here, and now they were fighting to keep it from driving them away.

"Whatever happens, Ford, I'm really glad I met you. You're the nicest cop I've ever met."

Another laugh grunted out of him. "You've never met any other cops."

She smiled big. "You've got me there. You're the first."

And what a first he was. She looked down at the badge clipped to his shirt. The mood shifted between them.

When she lifted her gaze, she saw the laughter in his eyes die away, to be replaced with fire. Licking flames ignited answering heat in her.

Before she could find the willpower to turn and bolt, he leaned down to kiss her. The soft touch stirred her desire. He moved over her mouth with only his lips at first, and then probed for more. She wrapped her arms over his shoulders, going up on her toes to accommodate him. He angled his head and delved into her, feeding her hunger and his own. She reveled in the sensations he elicited with the play of his tongue.

He withdrew and hovered over her. She touched his face and kissed his lips. His arms held her tighter. She dropped hers to his shoulders and let him kiss her deeply again. He lifted his head to look at her, and then kissed her yet again, endlessly making love to her with his mouth.

"Ford?" she breathed. This felt less urgent than the other times. But more intense.

In response, he lifted her, holding her rear on the strong curve of his arm. She wrapped her legs around him, aroused beyond comprehension as he carried her toward the stairs. Almost beyond comprehension.

"Not the stairs." She had enough control to make the request this time.

"I know," he rasped.

She kissed him all over his face as he climbed the stairs. In the hall, he stopped to press her against the wall. With her legs around him, she could feel the iron hardness of his erection. Flushed, she gripped his hair in her fist, breathing faster.

He reached for the hem of her top, pulling it up over her head and letting it fall to the floor. Lowering her legs, she tugged at his uniform pants while he opened her shorts.

"Your legs look really hot in these," he said.

"Your badge makes me hot." A symbol of what she loved about him, what she'd always love.

Lifting her again, he carried her into her bedroom and dropped her onto her fluffy comforter. She removed her bra and shimmied out of her underwear while he stood beside the bed and stripped off his uniform.

Then he was on the bed, between her legs and over her. He looked his fill at her body, as thrilling as an actual touch.

Then, slowly, savoring each second of this ecstasy, he lowered himself on top of her and kissed her with such meaning she lost herself to him.

She arched and opened her legs more.

"Gemma," he breathed. "What are we doing?"

"Just let it happen, Ford." She ran her hands over his shoulders, down his arms and back around to his butt.

He kissed her hard.

She expected him to do more, but he took his time. His kisses softened. He put his hands on each side of her face, caressed her with his thumbs.

After endless moments of excruciating anticipation, he rose up just enough to find her, sliding smoothly inside. He kept up his patient pace as he began to move back and forth. Riveting passion locked their gazes together. And then neither could stand it any longer. With a grunt, he moved faster, thrusting hard and sure. They came at the same time, an incredible peak rich with more than physical satisfaction.

As reason sank upon Gemma, she fought to pretend it didn't mean as much as it did. What hurt the most was seeing the same reaction in Ford.

But he rolled to his back and pulled her toward him. For tonight they'd forget the obstacle that would be there in the morning. And in the morning, she'd go get a pregnancy test.

Gemma found Ford standing on her front porch, watching across the street. Curiosity replaced the anxiety of facing him after last night and figuring out a way to get to the store without him. She stepped outside and saw Dillon loading luggage into the bed of his truck.

"His mother's home from the hospital," Ford said without turning toward her.

"Are they leaving?"

"For a while. Dillon agreed to leave the investigation up to me. He did the rest."

By convincing the three women to go with him. She searched for the car that had been parked in the street. It was gone. It hadn't been there yesterday, either. She wondered if Curtis's arrest had decided that tactic. Or had Samuel's strategy changed? She didn't like that option. What did he have up his cult-worshiped sleeve?

Hallie emerged with her grandmother, Martha, and Dillon rushed to his mother, who left the house after them.

"Let's go say goodbye," Ford said, stepping down the porch stairs.

"Why don't you? I need to run to the store real quick."

He stopped and turned. "What's your hurry?"

She shrugged. "No hurry."

"You're not going to say goodbye to your neighbor?"

After all they've been through, she could hear him thinking.

Damn.

Sighing, she hopped down the stairs and started walking.

"What do you need at the store?"

"Just some things."

She felt him eye her a bit before Hallie saw them and went to help Dillon's mother so that he could greet them. She took the injured woman to the truck while Dillon and Martha stepped up to Gemma and Ford.

Dillon extended his hand, and Ford shook it.

Gemma leaned to hug Martha. "I'll see you when you get back."

"Great goats, honey. I don't think I'll ever come back to this town." They moved back from the embrace. "As long as my Felix's murderer is caught, that will be all the memory I need of this place."

"I'll see to that," Ford said.

And Martha smiled, moisture pooling in her old eyes.

"Thanks for everything," Dillon said.

"I'll call you when I know something," Ford replied.

Dillon nodded.

Gemma walked toward the truck, giving Hallie a farewell hug before the girl went to stand beside Dillon and Ford.

Dillon's mom sat with her head resting against the seat. Gemma felt a need to talk to her, to offer support and encouragement. The woman lifted her head off the seat back when she approached, battered and bruised.

Gemma took her hand. "You have a wonderful son."

A smile glinted in her eyes. "Thank you. I know."

"You're lucky to have him, being married to someone abusive. If you ever need to talk, Martha has my number."

"Dillon told me about your ex-husband," she said.

"I'm sure the whole town knows about that."

"One more thing I won't miss about it."

"Maybe you should consider taking up baseball," Gemma quipped.

Dillon's mother laughed and then winced when the skin stretched too much, touching the side of her head as though it pained her. "So I can imagine Curtis's head is the ball."

"I spend my ex-husband's money on frivolous things because I know he would have hated it."

The other woman gave Gemma's hand a squeeze. "I'll take up baseball."

Stepping back, she waved and turned to see Ford saying goodbye to Hallie's grandmother.

"Gemma."

She turned to Dillon's mother again. "Don't let a good man pass you by because you made the mistake of marrying the wrong one."

Gemma smiled, wishing it were that simple. "I won't."

"I agree with her."

Pivoting, Gemma looked up at Dillon. "Take care of your mom." She didn't know what to say about Ford.

"Ford's a good man."

"I know." But would he walk away from a good woman? She hugged him. "Thanks."

"You, too."

Gemma went to stand beside Ford, waving to the four as Dillon climbed into his truck and Hallie got behind the wheel of her grandmother's car.

When the vehicles disappeared over a hill, quiet descended around them. Almost quiet. Birds chirped. Children laughed from some distant house. A dog barked.

And she was alone with Ford.

"I'll drive you to the store," he said, alarming her.

"Oh, you don't have to."

"I insist."

Lovely. Now she'd have to find a way to sneak the test

into the shopping cart and get through the checkout counter
without him noticing. Him. A cop…

At the beautiful and well-maintained natural foods market,
Gemma got a cart and pushed it toward the produce department. She put everything in the cart to make a salad, and
added bananas and apples. She needed a lot of groceries to
hide the test.

"We already have lettuce."

"I like salad."

Under his speculating gaze, she tossed another head of lettuce in the cart. In the meat section, she loaded up on crab
legs and salmon and headed for the frozen-food aisle. Pizza.
Burritos. Frozen dinners. The cart was a quarter full now.
She headed down the snack aisle. Crackers. Chips. Dips.

"Hungry?"

She caught his now very intrigued look and went to the
bakery and put in a few different kinds of bread. French.
Onion rolls. Sandwich bread. Plenty of places to hide a pregnancy test now. She went down the canned food aisle for good
measure.

"Are you going to fit all this in your kitchen?"

He was entertained by this. He probably thought she was
on a spending spree again.

After the juice aisle, they turned down the personal hy-
giene aisle. Seeing the tests just beyond the pads and tampons, she stopped and looked at Ford.

"Could you give me some privacy here?"

He looked from her to the pads and tampons and in typical
male fashion, experienced a moment of awkwardness before
nodding. "Sure." He turned. "Meet you in the next aisle."

She smiled at his retreating back, rolling the cart to the
tampons and then moving it to the pregnancy tests when he
disappeared.

Grabbing one, she tucked it under a box of crackers and

rolled the cart to the next aisle, where he looked at her from his study of toilet paper. She grabbed the most expensive package and put it on top of the crackers.

"Do you need anything?" she asked.

"No. I think you've got it covered."

She had it covered all right.

He followed her to the checkout counter. Her heartbeat pecked away at her ribcage. Maybe it would be easier if she just told him she thought she was pregnant. The reminder that his wife had died during childbirth and the infant boy hadn't survived quelled that idea.

The grocery clerk began checking out the contents of the cart. Ford stood beside her, watching. The clerk picked up the toilet paper. Next came the chips. A few cans of beans and tomatoes. Soup. Bread.

She reached for the crackers.

Gemma lifted a magazine and shoved it in front of Ford as the clerk ran the crackers through. The container of apple juice fell over onto the test.

"Another star gets divorced," Ford said, eyeing her peculiarly. He was starting to get suspicious.

His badge caught her attention and she got an idea. Seeing the clerk reach for the test, she touched the badge. His head lowered to look there and then his eyes lifted. As the pregnancy test made its way from the clerk's hand to the rolling belt, she moved so that Ford moved with her, his back to the counter.

"What are you doing?" he asked.

"Just reminiscing." She traced the edges of the badge as the pregnancy test waited for the bagger to pick it up.

Hurry!

"Reminiscing about what?"

"You know." She stepped closer to him, looking up at him suggestively. "Last night?"

He put his hands on her arms and moved her away from

him. "What's the matter with you?" He glanced back at the clerk, who'd slowed in the process of checking out the items to eye them.

He turned to face the counter. Gemma stopped breathing. The test was at the end of the counter. Ford's head began to move in that direction. The bagger lifted the test.

It disappeared inside the bag.

Ford hadn't seen it. Gemma breathed several times.

He glanced at her from under lowered brows. She wiped her forehead and smiled at him.

Now all she had to do was get him out of the kitchen while she unloaded the groceries.

Alone in the bathroom, Gemma unwrapped the pregnancy test. It had taken a near argument to get Ford to leave the kitchen. He offered to help her unload all the groceries but she'd refused. She'd almost had to yell at him. He hadn't understood. He didn't know why she was acting so weird. But he was curious enough to make her wonder if he wasn't starting to catch on.

Feeling pale and sick with foreboding, she performed the test and waited. When the pink plus sign appeared, a tremor shook her hand as she stared at it.

How would he feel about this? Would he be happy? Was she?

Pregnant.

Oh, dear Lord.

With Ford's baby. A feeling of pure euphoria stole over her before doubt chased it away again. How on earth was she going to tell him? She didn't trust his reaction. But he had to know. Didn't he? What if she waited a while?

No. Insecurities drove that impulse. Insecurity would keep her from taking the bold act of telling him what he had a right to know. Besides that, he was as much to blame for this as she.

Still, her legs felt shaky as she left the bathroom and made her way downstairs.

Ford was in the kitchen, sitting at the table drinking the new kind of soda she'd piled into the cart.

"It's pretty good." He held up the bottle.

Her nervous heartbeat made her swallow hard and catch her breath.

Noticing, he grew alert. "What's the matter?"

There was no avoiding it now. Gripping the test in her hand, she moved to the table and sat down across from him. Then she just sat there and stared at him.

He watched her, the first signs of uneasiness edging into his gaze.

Words clogged in her throat. Lifting the test, she opened her palm and extended it to him. He looked down, up and back down again.

"I thought you were on the Pill."

Disappointment plummeted inside her. "You never asked, so how could you know?"

"Women take care of that sort of thing. I thought you did... take care of it, I mean."

"Well, you thought wrong," she almost snapped. "Why is it up to the woman to do that?"

"I thought you'd tell me if you were worried about this happening. Most women do."

"Well, most women don't divorce an abusive husband! I wasn't even thinking about being with a man when you came along. This is as much your fault as it is mine!" She was so upset that he wasn't happy. Those brief seconds of euphoria she had had were obliterated now. He was going to let his fear take over, ruin any chance they had for happiness. If she weren't pregnant, she'd walk out on him right now.

Knocking brought them both to attention.

Ford stood up and went to the door. After peering through the peephole, he turned to look back at her. "It's Grayson."

Samuel? What did he want?

Removing his gun from the holster at his side, Ford checked its readiness and put it back into the holster. Then he opened the door, searching beyond Samuel. He was alone.

"Hello, Ford. I'm here to see Gemma."

Ford eyed him dubiously.

"May I come in?"

Ford opened the door wider and stepped aside, his movements mocking.

Samuel approached Gemma. "You're looking well."

"Thanks. What brings you here?"

"Is there somewhere we can talk?" He glanced back at Ford. "Alone?"

He wanted her alone so he could work his magic on her. "Anything you have to say Ford can hear."

Fleeting disapproval crossed his eyes. "I noticed you haven't been attending any seminars and I wanted to make sure you were all right. I strive to provide the community with the best therapy possible. I'm concerned over why I haven't seen you at the center."

Make sure she was all right? Therapy? She met Ford's silent scoff before turning back to him. "I'm fine. Why were you concerned?"

"I thought the seminars were helping you."

She folded her arms. "The seminars did help me, Samuel. But I don't need them anymore."

Samuel looked down at her folded arms briefly. "Are you certain? So soon?"

So soon. Meaning, he hadn't had enough time to brainwash her. "I'm certain."

He studied her, leashed frustration hidden behind the curtain of larger-than-life magnetism and good looks. "Is there something I should know about? Something that didn't meet with your expectations?"

Ford moved as smoothly as a protective angel around Samuel.

"No. The seminars did help me. Really." Ford stood beside her now. "I just don't need them anymore." As she'd already said.

He smiled, congenial and infectious, presenting a man with selfless benevolence that expertly cloaked his true intent. "I have a special interest in you, Gemma. A woman like you sets a fine example. You've been given difficult mental hardships to overcome, but you've persevered. You've begun to make a new life here, one people can look up to. I would hate to see you endure any more setbacks."

Wow. The veiled threat was barely discernable. His special interest nauseated her. And she didn't delude herself that her bracelet turning up at Jed's crime scene was one of the setbacks he referred to. Would there be more if she didn't cooperate? Didn't yield to his ways and become a Devotee?

She glanced over at Ford, who wore a smirk.

"I appreciate all you've done, Samuel, and for thinking so highly of me. But you won't see me at the community center anymore."

He flashed an accusatory look at Ford. "I encourage you to reconsider."

"And I encourage you to stop pressuring me."

Now he had the opportunity to catch her own veiled threat. "Perhaps if you spent some time away from local law enforcement you'd change your mind."

"Asking Ford to watch over me was the best decision you made. I feel so safe when I'm with him." She put her arm around him and he put his around her.

The blatant snub brewed anger in Samuel's gaze. "Very well. Then my worry is eased." He went to the door with one last look at both of them. "Good day."

Ford shut the door and faced her.

"I can't wait to find out what they'll do next," she said.

"We need to find who killed Jed and the others before that happens."

How? Bo had taken the best chance of that when he took the laptop.

They stood in her living room staring at each other. It wasn't long before the magnitude of their earlier conversation returned.

Ford moved away from her, awkward again. Though he wouldn't admit he was afraid, fear billowed from him. That's why he'd claimed to want to wait until he was in his forties to have a family again. Avoidance was his motto. The prospect of fathering another baby terrified him.

His cell phone rang. Another interruption.

Gemma folded her arms again, this time rubbing them. What was she going to do?

"McCall." He listened, and then, "Excellent. Your timing couldn't be better. I'm on my way."

He tucked his phone away.

"Where are we going?"

"I'm going. You're staying here."

He was leaving her? "What about Samuel?"

"You'll be all right."

Somehow she doubted that. His judgment was fogged by the knowledge that she was pregnant. In the next instant, she realized she didn't care. If he could abandon her that easily, then she didn't want him anywhere near her.

"Fine. Go, then. But don't come back here when you're finished."

Stunned, he stared at her. "Gemma, I can't take you."

"You could if you wanted to."

After a long, searching look, her ultimatum slid behind a barrier. Cutting himself off from her, he turned and left, taking her heart with him.

Gemma tipped her head back and breathed through the tears that burned her eyes. *How could he?*

How could he walk out on her after learning she was pregnant with their child? So they barely knew each other. They'd created a life together. Would he walk out on that, too?

This couldn't have gone worse. She'd worried he'd take the news hard, but walking out on her? And right after she'd turned Samuel away. A tear swelled over her lid, tickling her skin on its way down her cheek. She angrily swiped it away.

She wished she could have stayed away from him. Even if she'd thought to go on the Pill or make him wear protection, she wouldn't have before that first time on the stairs. That had happened without warning. Neither of them could have prevented it. And unfortunately, she was pretty sure that's when he'd gotten her pregnant.

Gemma swiped another tear away, plopping down on one of her living-room chairs and hanging her head low. She was well on her way to ending up just like her mother. Single and with a lover who couldn't step up to the plate and be a father.

Chapter 12

Ford saw the dark Audi following him and took a turn before leaving town. His errand would have to wait. He drove back to Main Street and parked in front of Cold Plains Coffee. Getting out of his SUV, he spotted the Audi parking down the street. Bo got out of the passenger side. The tall and lanky Wade Herrington was driving. What was he doing with Bo?

Entering the coffee shop, he spotted Alan talking urgently to one of Lacy's workers. He didn't see Lacy. Alan turned and saw him just as Bo entered the shop with Herrington, thin blond hair combed neatly back and ghostly gray eyes scanning the crowd, lingering on Ford.

Herrington sat down at a table by himself and Bo walked toward Ford. Alan reached him first.

"Have you seen Lacy?" the burly man asked.

"No." He glanced toward the counter and saw Lacy's workers talking anxiously amongst themselves, haphazardly serving customers.

"Are you sure? She and Gemma are good friends. Has she heard from her? Is she staying with you?"

Ford couldn't decide if Alan was worried or angry. Maybe both. He wanted to find Lacy, but why? And why was she suddenly missing? "Why would she be staying at Gemma's house?"

"Where is she?" Alan demanded.

"What happened? Why are you looking for Lacy?" Ford asked.

"She's been missing for two days," Bo said, coming to a stop before them. "Are you sure you don't know where she went?"

The way he asked said he thought Ford did know. "Neither Gemma nor I have seen her in almost a week. What'd she do? Run away from Grayson?"

Bo scrutinized him for several seconds, and then let the issue drop, putting a copy of today's Cold Plains newspaper on the table beside them. On the front was a photo of Gemma and Ford coming out of the grocery store. This was the reason he'd followed him here. He didn't care about Lacy. Neither did Grayson.

Ford read the headline of the local paper: Witness Comes Forth in Jed Johnson Case.

"Something come up?" he queried without reading further.

"David Retting over at the Stillwater stopped by the station yesterday. Turns out he saw Gemma leaving Jed's room the night of his murder, just before he went in and found the body."

Ford couldn't even muster up the motivation to appear surprised. "I take it Grayson accurately predicted what Gemma's answer would be this morning." He hadn't even waited until after his visit to print the article.

They must have been on the way to Gemma's house when they'd spotted him and followed. What had they intended to do? Arrest her? Maybe they hadn't anticipated he'd leave her alone. He shouldn't have. He'd let his emotions make that decision. Finding out she was pregnant had really knocked his sensibilities. He hadn't expected it. Hadn't seen it coming. And yet, he should have. Gemma was right about that. This was as much his fault as hers.

"We'd like you to bring her in, Ford," Bo said.

"Me?"

"If you don't, we will."

Is that what they'd been on their way to tell him? Did Grayson want to make him arrest her out of sick pleasure? Retaliation for going against him? He thought he had plenty of evidence against her. He thought Ford would have no choice.

"I'm not going to arrest her." He loomed over Bo, taller and a little bulkier. "You and I both know she didn't kill Jed."

"That's not how it appears. David Retting claims he saw her."

"Retting stole Jed's laptop before calling to report the murder. You remember…the laptop you took from the forensic lab?"

"There was no laptop at the scene."

"I suppose you also don't know anything about the forensics technician, either. He saw the recording. Did he identify the killer? Is that why you had him murdered?"

Murmurs spread through the coffee shop.

"Those are some serious allegations, McCall. Can you back them up?"

The technician had been hanged like all the others, but there'd been no baseball bat. If he could link the rope to the other murders, he could very easily back up his allegations. Bo felt untouchable, just like Samuel. Just like the hit man committing murders in the name of health and prosperity. Ford needed them all to sweat a little. Long enough for him to spare Gemma any time in jail, or anything worse they had in store for her.

"What if I could?" he asked.

Bo searched for a bluff. He wouldn't see any signs of one. "You can't prove anything."

"The murders are stacking up," Ford said. "And they have a few things in common."

"What's that?"

"I think you already know the answer to that."

Once again, Bo engaged in a stare-down with Ford.

Bo became uncertain now. "What have you got, Ford?"

"Michael, the technician. Jed. And Felix. And that poor man who had the misfortune of living too close to the location where Felix's body was found. All of them were knocked unconscious before they were hanged. I hope you didn't have anything to do with that."

Bo's uncertainty vanished. "You don't have anything. If you did, you'd have already made the arrests. I know you better than you think I do. You're a lawman first. Arrest Gemma. Do it and you can keep your job." He glanced over at Alan and gave a nod. Alan reluctantly turned with the silent command and left the coffee shop.

"I'm not arresting her." Ford stepped close to Bo. "And you don't have to hold my job over my head. I quit." Bumping his ex-boss's shoulder as he passed, he left the coffee shop and strode to his SUV. He had a bad feeling about this. A really bad feeling. He never should have left Gemma alone.

Driving away from the coffee shop, he got about three blocks before two other Escalades appeared behind him. He cursed and floored the SUV. He had to get to Gemma before they did.

Gemma paced from her living room to the kitchen. Each time she did, she saw the newspaper. She didn't get the paper delivered. Someone had dropped it outside her door after Ford had left. Someone who'd wanted her to see it.

Where was Ford? Would she be arrested for Jed's murder? Imagining herself in prison, she felt chilled and bloodless.

Someone rang her doorbell, giving her a jolt. Would Ford ring it? Or would he walk right in?

She went to the peephole.

Bo Fargo and another man stood there. He looked familiar. Samuel's second in command, Wade Herrington. She breathed faster with foreboding.

"Oh, God," she whispered.

"Gemma Johnson?" Bo called. "Open up."

Stepping back from the door, she turned in a circle. What should she do? Should she run to her car and try to escape? Should she call Ford?

The door was bashed in.

Gemma screamed as Wade and Bo stepped over splintered wood. She turned to run for her back door, but Wade caught her, taking hold of her arm and roughly hauling her back against him.

Bo approached with handcuffs.

"No!" she protested.

"You're under arrest for the murder of Jed Johnson." He clasped one side of the cuffs to her wrist and Wade forced her to turn as he secured the other behind her back.

Dizzy with fear, Gemma barely heard as he recited her rights.

Wade left her house ahead of them and Bo pushed her forward to follow.

"What are you doing?" Gemma struggled against Bo when he grasped her.

Wade opened the back of a black Audi. Why wasn't it a real police car? This didn't feel right.

Bo put his hand on the top of her head and forced her into the back seat. After he got in the front seat, Wade began driving toward town.

"You won't get away with this." She frantically searched for signs of Ford's Escalade. *Where was he?*

"No, I believe you're the one who isn't going to get away with something," Bo said. "You killed your ex-husband."

Eerily, Wade didn't say anything. Only his creepy light gray eyes shifted to the rearview mirror every once in a while.

"That's not true. You're only doing this because I refused to join Samuel's cult!"

"There's no cult in Cold Plains, Gemma. Only peace-loving people. People like you just don't belong here. You had us all fooled, didn't you?"

"You're crazy! Ford will prove I'm innocent."

Bo chuckled and Wade looked at her again. What was he doing with Bo anyway? Making sure he did Samuel's bidding?

Wade pulled to a stop in front of the police station.

"I'll take it from here," Bo said to him. "Tell Samuel everything's under control."

The tall, Lurch look-alike gave a nod and Bo climbed out of the Audi. Opening the back door, he grabbed Gemma's arm and slid her to the edge of the seat. She stumbled out of the car, Bo steadying her.

The Audi drove away. A man in a suit left the building and a car backed out of a parking space. Other than that, it was quiet. The man in the suit glanced at them and went on his way.

Bo forced her into the police station, down familiar hallways and then to a not-so-familiar stairway. At the bottom, he took her to a row of cells and stopped at one of them.

"Please don't lock me in there." She couldn't control her fear. If Ford couldn't save her, what would happen to her?

Removing her cuffs, he said, "It didn't have to be this way, you know. Samuel was very fond of you. He had such hopes for you. It isn't often a woman like you comes along, someone who seems so together. So willing to improve. You've disappointed him beyond recovery."

"You're arresting me for something I didn't do!"

"Alert the media." Chuckling, he shoved her into the cell and slammed the door closed.

She fell against the cot and pushed back to her feet, gripping the bars. "You can't keep me in here!" She searched the other cells. They were all empty. "I'm supposed to get a call!"

Bo kept walking away.

"Hey!"

"You won't have long to wait, dear Gemma."

Wait for what? Would she be brought to the community center, taken to that secret place she'd only heard about until now? Is that where she'd disappear? Would Samuel arrange to have her killed? Or would Bo have her prosecuted for murder and send her off to prison?

Backing away from the bars, she put her hand on her stomach. She hated the thought of having a baby in prison. Would Samuel kill her if he knew she was pregnant? He didn't like Ford. Maybe that wouldn't matter.

Trembling, sick to her stomach, Gemma sat on the cot and hugged her knees. All she could do now was wait. And hope Ford would come and get her.

Ford.

Would he come for her?

When Ford reached the outskirts of town, he began to worry. He'd been unable to lose the two Escalades behind him. Alan and the other henchmen were good.

Suddenly the first Escalade closed ground on him. Kept coming. Ford sped up. So did the other Escalade, the second one close behind. The first one ran into his bumper. The other drove up beside him. Ford yanked his wheel, ramming the other SUV and sending it veering off to the left. Ford pulled his cell phone out to call Hawk. The SUV behind him ran into his bumper again. Dropping his phone, he fought to stay in control. He swerved and straightened, but not in time to deflect the second SUV as it rammed into him. He swerved again and went off the road.

The other two SUVs cornered him. He had nowhere to go. Climbing out of the driver's seat, he pulled his gun just as one of the other men appeared and hit him in the head.

Ford blocked the next strike and got in a few punches of his own. The man fell to the ground. But there were three others who now surrounded him.

He tried to aim his gun but one of them kicked his wrist while another slugged his sternum. He dropped his gun and swung his feet and fists, blocking as many attacks as he could. He was outnumbered. He knew he was in trouble when he began to black out.

Chapter 13

When Ford regained consciousness, he grew aware of movement. He was in a vehicle. The back of an Escalade. His Escalade. Rising up, he peered over the top of the back seat and saw a single driver. Alan.

Blood dripping from an open cut on his forehead caused him some worry. His ribs hurt. His head hurt. He was in bad shape. Those lackeys must have really gone the rounds with him after he'd lost consciousness. He wasn't even sure he had the strength to get out of his current situation.

The SUV stopped but Alan left it running. Ford waited until he came around to the back and opened it. Then he used both his legs to kick the man, ramming both feet to his middle. With a grunt of surprise and pain, Alan stumbled back.

Ford groaned as he climbed out of the SUV. Alan advanced for an attack. Blocking his punch with a forearm, Ford swung in low with his other arm to slam his fist against his sternum. As Alan staggered, Ford used his legs again, kicking high to knock the man's chin backward. Alan collapsed to the ground. Ford bent over him and pulled out the gun sticking out of his pants.

Blood ran down his head and he couldn't take very deep breaths. Alan must have noticed. He grabbed hold of his hand and tried to wrestle the gun from him. Ford fired and the man slumped.

Hunched over from pain, Ford saw that he was in the mountains at a pull-off on a sharp curve in the road where a cliff dropped down to a canyon. Had Bo tried to make Alan drive him over a cliff or would Alan have just thrown him over? If he hadn't regained consciousness in time…

Gemma.

More than physical pain gripped him as he stumbled toward the Escalade. He was such a fool. He should never have left her alone. No doubt Bo had arrested her. She'd have to wait for him in jail. He just hoped he could reach her in time before Grayson decided to do something else with her, other than accuse her of a murder she didn't commit.

Tripping over his own feet, Ford sank to his knees beside the Escalade. He needed to find Hawk Bledsoe. Since he'd missed their meeting, he didn't even know what the agent had for him. He hoped it was what he'd been waiting for, his secret ace. But he was no good to anyone like this.

Using the side of the SUV, he rose to his feet and made his way to the driver's door. He sat in the driver's seat, dropping the gun in his lap, and struggling to catch his breath. He needed help.

Pregnant. Gemma was pregnant. It slammed him now in the same way it had when she'd told him.

Leaning his head back, he felt the day he'd lost his wife push past the wall he'd kept sturdy and impenetrable until now. The day the doctors couldn't save his unborn baby. They'd gone to the hospital after she'd begun to have contractions. Everything fell apart from there. She'd developed an aneurysm and the doctors hadn't been able to save the baby in time. The unthinkable had happened: he'd gone from having a wife and a baby on the way to nothing.

The doctor had emerged from the operating room, blood on his gown.

I'm sorry to have to tell you this...

Incomprehensible agony gripped him. He felt it now as clearly as though it were happening all over again. Happiness ripped from his chest. A future he had yearned to experience, taken from him.

For weeks he'd gone through life just existing, drowning in grief so great he sometimes wondered if he'd be better off dead. He would never have gotten her pregnant if he'd known it would kill her. And the baby. It was bad enough to have lost her. Why did he have to lose them both?

Anger had spared him. Anger had cleansed the grief. He'd lost his family to murder and a wife to childbirth. Why?

He realized then that Gemma had been the first woman he hadn't been vigilant with when it came to birth control. The chemistry was so explosive with her, he could see now that it had been easy for him to turn a blind eye. He'd reassured himself that she surely was on the Pill, or something. He was sure she'd have mentioned something to him. But after that first time he'd known, deep down, that it was different with her.

Amazingly, there was still a part of him that yearned to have a family again. He hadn't given up. As painful as it was to risk losing another person he loved, Gemma was going to be worth it. He loved her. Like the first time they'd had sex, that love had emerged unexpectedly. Instantly.

She'd been right when she'd said he was afraid. But not anymore. He hoped it wasn't too late.

Hearing a car approach, he didn't put the Escalade into gear. He couldn't see very well and he felt as though he'd black out. He needed more time to regain his strength and equilibrium. If more of Grayson's men were coming for him, he was in trouble.

A car pulled up next to him. He blinked but couldn't see clearly. A man got out and started to walk toward him.

Ford picked up the gun from his lap just as the man appeared beside the window. It was Hawk, tall and muscular, dark blond hair waving in a breeze and brown eyes hidden by sunglasses.

"I'm glad you left your cell phone on." Hawk opened the door and helped Ford to the other side, belting him in and then hurrying to the driver's side. Then he raced the Escalade back toward Cold Plains.

"When you didn't show up at our meeting place, I knew something had gone wrong."

"They arrested Gemma. I tried to stop them."

"I know. But they won't be able to keep her." With one hand on the wheel, Hawk dug into his suit-jacket pocket and handed over a CD inside a clear plastic case. The CD wasn't marked but Ford didn't need it to be. He knew what it was.

He took the CD from Hawk. "Take me to the station."

"You need a doctor first. Gemma is fine. I checked on her. She's in a jail cell and nobody's going to move her."

Ford didn't ask how he'd checked on her. Hawk no doubt had other contacts inside the police department. "Take me to Rafe Black. I don't trust anyone else." Ford shut his eyes as Hawk made a call and told Darcy Craven he was bringing a banged up Ford McCall for an emergency visit. Darcy was the receptionist there, and Rafe's fiancée.

When he disconnected, Hawk asked, "Have you talked to the hotel desk clerk?"

"No. I haven't had a chance. How'd you know about that?"

"I saw the paper. It's a lie."

The man didn't miss much and Ford couldn't be more grateful.

Hawk screeched to a halt in front of Rafe Black's office,

an old bungalow-style building set in a tree-lined parking lot with a few stairs leading to the entrance. Ford opened his door and Hawk came around to help him. He began to guide him toward the stairs, but Ford stopped and stepped away from his support.

"I'm okay. It's best if nobody sees you with me."

After a moment, Hawk nodded once. "I'll find my own way back to my car."

Ford didn't doubt the agent's resourcefulness. He started walking toward the street, taking out his cell phone as he did.

"Hawk."

Hawk turned.

"Thanks."

"Thank me after we have Grayson."

"I'll look forward to that."

As Hawk resumed his trek toward the street, Ford used the railing to help him up the stairs. Pushing the door open, he ignored two patients sitting in chairs who looked up in shock at the sight of him.

Darcy's beautiful blue eyes widened and she jumped up from her chair behind the reception desk. Something about her eyes struck him. They'd captured his notice before, as though they were familiar to him, reminded him of…who? Opening the door leading to the rooms, she went to him.

"Mr. McCall?" Darcy took his arm for support. "Hawk said you were banged up, not beaten to a pulp."

Doc Black's nurse appeared in the hall from one of the rooms and saw him. "Bring him in here, Darcy." She pointed to the room across the hall.

Ford entered the room and sat on the paper-covered table.

The nurse began checking him out, examining his head. "You've got a pretty good gash here."

"Could you go get Doc Black?" Ford couldn't be here long.

"I'll do it," Darcy said, and Ford realized she was still in the room.

Moments later, Rafe entered. "What happened to you?"

"I was jumped by Grayson's thugs. They drove me off the road and four of them were on me."

Rafe began examining him and then asked his nurse to bring everything he needed to suture him up.

"You've got some pretty deep bruises." He pressed his ribs and Ford winced. "Maybe a fractured rib or two. Once we get you stitched you should go home and recover for a few days."

First he had to go get Gemma.

The nurse returned and handed Rafe what he needed, and Darcy appeared with a blank chart, putting it on the counter adjacent to the table. Then she stayed, watching Rafe work on Ford.

When Rafe had finished, he wheeled his chair to the counter and began writing in the chart.

"I'll take it from here, Kelly," Darcy said to the nurse.

"Thanks. We've got a lot of patients to see." The nurse left the room. Given Darcy's intimate relationship with Rafe, she was in a position of power here at his office.

Darcy began washing him, wiping the skin of his face. "I've been meaning to ask you something."

"What is it?"

"I need to know how to find someone who's missing."

Why did she need to know that? "Is someone you know missing?" Another one? This was getting to be a regular occurrence.

She glanced over at Rafe, who'd stopped writing in the chart. He gave her a nod.

Turning back to Ford, she said, "Yes. My mother. Her name is Catherine."

"Catherine...?"

"I don't have a last name."

No last name. "You don't know your mother's name?"

"She didn't raise me. She...gave me up when I was a baby."

Ah. She was an adopted child looking for her biological mother. "Catherine is a common name. You might try death records and hospitals where she went missing. I can't guarantee you'll find anything." And then something came to him. "Why do you say she's missing?"

"Well, I…I can't find her."

Ford studied her for a while. She wasn't telling him everything. And then he realized why her eyes were so familiar to him. They could be similar to Jane Doe's. The computer-enhanced photo was a close likeness, close enough to put him on full alert.

He pulled out the photo he always carried in his wallet and showed it to her. "Have you ever seen this woman before?"

With a sharply indrawn breath, Darcy took the photo from him. "Her eyes."

"It's a computer-enhanced photo of a Jane Doe I've been trying to find. Do you recognize her?"

"No, but…"

"Do you think this could be your mother?" The age difference between the two was just about right.

Darcy studied the photo some more. "She does look a lot like me. But…isn't this woman dead?"

"Yes." He told her the woman was found in the woods outside of town, and that she'd been shot. "She had a *D* marked on her hip."

With that, Darcy's stunning blue eyes flashed to his.

"Not a tattoo, a marker was used," Ford stressed.

"Do you think she was pretending to be a Devotee?"

"That's what we suspect."

Darcy's perplexed state creased her brow. "Why?"

"We don't know. Are you sure you only know her first name?"

Crestfallen, Darcy handed him back the photo, nodding. "That could be my mother."

"I'm sorry, Darcy." If Jane Doe was Darcy's mother, she'd

have to face the realization Catherine was dead. "I'll let you know if I find anything new about the case."

If Jane Doe's name was Catherine, he was one more step closer to identifying her.

Gemma lifted her head when she heard the sound of voices. Hours had passed.

"Sir! You can't go down here! Chief Fargo left specific instructions."

"Tell the chief I'm here and I need to talk to him. But first, I'm letting Gemma out of that cell."

"I can't let you do—"

The sound of shuffling and a fleshy punch matched shadows on the wall. Then Ford came into view. He threw a man onto the floor and stepped over him on his way to Gemma's cell. Her sexy cop was here to rescue her! Except he wasn't looking very sexy right now.

"Ford?" His face was battered and he wasn't moving with his usual smooth stride. He seemed to be in a fair amount of pain. "What happened to you?"

"Sorry it took me so long. I ran into trouble and then I had a few things I had to do first." He was all business as he unlocked the cell. But his shallow breathing told her his business had more to do with moving right now. Unlocking the cell, he took her hand and hauled her into the aisle.

"Who did that to you?" And then that seemed like a stupid question. Bo had sent someone after him. Had they tried to silence him for good?

The junior officer had gotten to his feet and now watched them pass, rubbing his mouth.

"What are we going to do?"

"You'll see."

Upstairs, he led her hand-in-hand into his office area, off

which was a small meeting room. Inside, he pulled out a chair for her.

Puzzled, she sat down.

He turned on the overhead projector and logged on to the computer. As the screen loaded, Bo appeared.

"What the hell do you think you're doing?" He entered the meeting room with two officers close behind, aiming their weapons at Gemma and Ford.

Gemma gripped the armrests of her chair, staring at the end of a pistol. She hoped whatever Ford had was good.

"I have evidence that proves Gemma's innocence," he told the three, holding up a CD. Bending, he pressed a button on the front of the computer that resided under the table and inserted the disc.

"You no longer work here. You quit, remember? You don't belong here anymore." Bo turned to the cop beside him. "Arrest him!"

As Gemma gaped at Ford with the news that he'd quit, two more policemen appeared, forcing in Wade Herrington, who'd been cuffed.

"We found him, Ford," one of the officers said. His partner pulled out a chair at the end of the table, away from Gemma, and forced Wade to sit.

"You're all going to pay for this!" Wade growled. His haughty blustering promised backing from Samuel.

The officer who'd forced Wade to sit moved around the table to Ford and handed him a folder. "After you got the warrant, we searched his house and found this."

Ford took it and read through the contents. "Good work." He smiled at the officers and put the folder down on the table.

"You better have a good reason for this," Bo hissed.

"Watch." Ford pointed to the screen.

The video recording of Jed's murder began to play, only this one had been adjusted so that the picture was clearer.

When the man appeared in front of the camera, his image was recognizable.

Gemma shot a look over at Wade, who wasn't looking so haughty anymore. He gaped at the screen, and then sent an accusatory look toward Bo.

"There are more copies," Ford said, "So don't even consider trying to destroy this one."

"How did you…?" Bo was clearly baffled.

So was Gemma. Where had he gotten this recording? Had he found the laptop?

"Before I took the laptop to the lab, I made a copy."

Gemma should have realized the possibility. He must have given a copy to his friend with the FBI and they'd cleaned up the pixels to make Wade identifiable. He'd used the forensics technician but kept his backup plan a secret.

"Lower your weapons," Ford told the officers Bo had brought in. Those two glanced at the chief, who nodded reluctantly, his irritation burgeoning. He had to be getting tired of Ford's interference.

They lowered their guns.

With his fingers on the folder, Ford slid it down the table as he walked to Wade. "I would think a man of your expertise would be more careful. Or did you think you were infallible with Grayson supporting you?"

"I don't know what you're talking about."

Opening the folder, Ford showed him the first piece of paper. "This is a copy of your credit card statement. You made a purchase at a hardware store in Shady Meadow the day before Felix Taylor was murdered. You bought some rope and a baseball bat there."

"What we believe are rope fibers were found in his vehicle," the officer closest to Wade said. "We sent them in for analysis."

Ford turned to Wade. "Do you think they'll match the rope used at the other scenes? The lab technician? Felix

Taylor? The man from Shady Meadow?" He paused. "Jed Johnson?"

In the face of such overwhelming evidence, Wade only glared back at him. Ford wondered how he felt about Grayson now. All the crimes would be pinned to him, not Grayson. He'd believed in Grayson and the cult, felt he had power. Now that power had been stripped from him.

Ford turned to the officers he'd brought in. "Take him away." Then he walked around the table to Gemma, reaching for her hand.

She took it and stood, backing against him.

"Once again I have to commend you, McCall," Bo said. The compliment must taste like blood on his tongue. "You solved Jed Johnson's murder and maybe three others. Gemma is free to go."

He knew when he had to back down.

"I've sent some officers to arrest the henchmen who chased me down this afternoon," Ford said. "Except Alan won't be among them. He decided dying was better than failing to send me over a cliff."

Bo held a blank gaze.

"I'll want to question the hotel desk clerk. Any idea where he is?"

"I don't know. Have you tried his home?"

"Yes, as a matter of fact, I stopped by there on my way here. He wasn't there, but his car was still in his garage. There was an uneaten pizza on top of his oven. Looked like someone snatched him right before he was about to have dinner."

"Maybe he decided to skip dinner before going on vacation."

"A lot of people seem to be doing that lately, going on vacation without telling anyone. Strange, don't you think?"

"Very." Bo did an amazing job of hiding his emotion, when he had to be stewing inside.

Ford had struck a deep blow catching Wade, but he had yet to gain the grand prize.

Chapter 14

Lights dotted the nearly empty parking lot outside the police station; the night was windless and quiet. Walking beside Ford, Gemma felt the illusion of peace settle over Cold Plains. She no longer had to worry about being accused of Jed's murder and Ford no longer worked for Bo. Their ties to Samuel were severed. He had nothing to hold against them. But there was still the matter of the five unsolved murders, Jane Doe's in particular. Now that Ford had decided to take his experience and put it into P.I. work, would he still pursue the case?

"What are you going to do now?" she asked.

"I was thinking of dinner in tonight." He put a hand on his ribs and grimaced.

"Or a hospital?"

"Dinner in. With you." He stopped walking and faced her.

Gemma stopped, too, wary of his meaning. She hadn't forgotten that he'd walked out on her. "I was actually talking about *you*. You quit your job."

"I've got some money saved. I'll open my own private investigation office in town."

"Samuel might not like that."

"There's nothing he can do to stop me."

"Yes, I think by now he knows you're an opponent he can't win against. If you stay out of his way, he'll stay out of yours."

"I'll stay out of his way until I have evidence against him. Bo, too."

So, he wasn't going to stop looking into the Jane Doe case. She wasn't surprised. Ford wasn't a quitter, especially when it came to the law. He had his future all planned. What was she going to do? Stay in Cold Plains? Move?

With a baby on the way.

Saddened, she looked toward the front of the well-lit police station. No one exited. More illusionary peace. Her inner peace was beginning to fall apart.

"Gemma." Ford moved closer and took her hands in his. "I was wrong to walk out on you," he said. "You were right about me. I tried to avoid falling in love. But the truth is, I have. And I'm terrified of you having a baby, but there's nothing on this planet that I want more."

Numbed by what he'd said, Gemma had trouble responding. "Ford…" If he wasn't sure about this, then they'd come up with some kind of compromise. He didn't have to be with her if it wouldn't make him happy. She had lots of money now. Things would be different for her than they had been for her mother. And she'd raise her child with love and plenty of guidance.

"Please forgive me, Gemma," he said. "I was confused before. I'm not anymore. I've gone so long without a family, I don't know how to be a part of one anymore. Every semblance of family that I've ever had I've lost."

"I won't force you into anything. If you need time, that's

okay. I'll give you time. I'm not ready for this, either. Motherhood? Hell, I just got a divorce!"

His brow lowered in consternation. "I want to give this a try. Us. The baby…being a family."

Her heart pinged with bursting joy and apprehension. And then the echo of something he'd said pushed into her conscience.

"Wait a minute. Did I hear you say you've fallen in love with me?"

He grinned. "Don't look so shocked."

She breathed a laugh. "It's just… Earlier you…"

"Earlier I should have known what you were up to at the grocery store. I didn't want to accept it. I do now, Gemma. I want to be a father. A husband. More than anything, I want to have a family again."

"Ford…" She refrained from jumping against him. Was she being too impulsive in believing him? He had a lot to overcome. Like her.

Or did they?

"I know it's soon. We just met. But you're pregnant, so if you're willing…" he hedged.

Willing to do what? It could only be one thing. He was going to ask her to marry him. Too soon. But too right to say no. He was nothing like Jed. There was no comparison.

Meeting Ford had healed her. And meeting her had healed him enough to conquer his fear.

"Will you marry me?" he finally asked.

With a huge smile, she threw her arms around his neck. He lifted her against him, grunting with pain but holding her to him.

She covered his face with kisses. "Ford. Oh, Ford." Never had she been more sure about anything.

"Is that a yes?"

"Yes!" She kept kissing him.

He chuckled, low and deep. "Anna will be thrilled. We have a lot of news she's been waiting a long time to hear."

Gemma burst with excitement. "I can't wait to get to know her. Take me to see her like she asked." When his work was finished. It was finished now.

"Let's go home and call her."

"We can convert the guest room into an office. You can use it to start your business."

"It'll be nice to get out of that apartment."

Her home was now their home. Cold Plains wasn't a fairy tale for her anymore, but she'd have her own with Ford. Their house. Their family. Kissing him once more, she paid no attention to the car that had pulled to a stop along the curb.

"I'm going to love redecorating." She kissed him some more. She'd also love to donate a good chunk of Jed's money to charities for abused women.

"I'm going to love you."

She laughed lightly and kept kissing him as a car door shut and footsteps drew closer. A man clearing his throat broke them apart. He was tall and well-built like Ford, with medium blond hair and brown eyes.

"I thought I'd find you here," he said to Ford.

"Hawk Bledsoe." Ford told Gemma. "The agent I told you about."

"Gemma Johnson." She stuck out her hand. "Thank you for helping Ford."

He took her hand. "He didn't need much."

Ford glanced back at the police station and then surveyed the parking lot as though looked for something amiss. "What are you doing here?"

"Rafe called me a few minutes ago. He asked me to tell you his son's just been kidnapped."

Kidnapped? She'd heard the boy had been missing before. How had he turned up missing again?

"He didn't call it in," Hawk continued. "Bo might interfere. As you can imagine, he's out of his mind with worry."

"I'll see what I can do."

And Gemma knew he would.

Hawk gave a nod. "I assume you've heard about Lacy Matthews by now?"

Lacy? What had happened to Lacy? Apprehension rose in Gemma. She moved closer to Ford and put her hands on his back and chest. Was Lacy all right?

Ford put his arm around her. "Yes. I planned to check into that, too."

Hawk noticed how close they stood while she looked at Ford in question. He knew?

"I was on my way to meet Hawk when Bo started following me. I stopped at Cold Plains Coffee," he explained. "Alan was there, looking for Lacy. She's been missing for two days."

Gemma inhaled along with the chill that news triggered. This town had a bad case of missing persons. Would it ever end?

"We've started a search with local police," Hawk said.

"What could have happened to her? Has someone taken her and the girls?" Why would anyone do that?

"Either that or she ran," Ford said.

From Samuel. Could it be? Had Lacy turned against Samuel and his cult? Was she no longer under his influence? That made the most sense to Gemma. But had Lacy fled, or were she and her girls the newest Cold Plains murder victims?

A shiver racked her.

Ford rubbed her arm to comfort her.

"Do you have any leads?" she asked Hawk. "Did anyone see her two days ago?"

"A pair of red shoes was found in the woods not far from here. We've confirmed they belong to one of Lacy's twins, but I'm afraid that's all we've got right now."

"I remember her showing them to me." She'd been so excited to bring them home to her girls. She tipped her head up to see Ford. "Who would hurt two three-year-old girls?"

"Maybe they ran away, Gemma. Others have."

She rested her head on the pad of his chest, wishing she knew he was right. He rubbed her arm some more, defusing her tension.

Once again, Hawk took note of the intimate contact. "One of the officers helping with the search told me you quit your job today. I think he was glad to hear it."

Ford wasn't the only officer on the force who suspected Bo was corrupt.

"He's starting a P.I. business." Gemma gazed up at Ford with a smile that Hawk noticed.

"Looks like that's not all he's started."

Gemma laughed. "You have no idea." She was pregnant and they were getting married.

"Congratulations." He turned to Ford. "I'll let you two recover from all you've been through. Let's stay in touch."

"Thanks. I'm nowhere near finished with Grayson."

Gemma waved her farewell after Ford shook Hawk's hand. The agent walked away.

"Let's go home," Ford said.

Nothing sounded sweeter. Never once had she anticipated escaping a violent ex-husband only to fall into the arms of a cop who far exceeded all she'd ever dreamed of finding in a man. All the disasters of Cold Plains dropped away with the prospect of a new future with Ford. She was going to cherish her life with him every day. And she'd do everything she could to outlive him, protect their child from harm and see that he never knew loss again.

* * * * *

SUSPENSE

Harlequin® ROMANTIC
SUSPENSE

COMING NEXT MONTH
AVAILABLE APRIL 24, 2012

#1703 HER HERO AFTER DARK
H.O.T. Watch
Cindy Dees

#1704 THE PERFECT OUTSIDER
Perfect, Wyoming
Loreth Anne White

#1705 TEXAS MANHUNT
Chance, Texas
Linda Conrad

#1706 IT STARTED THAT NIGHT
Virna DePaul

REQUEST YOUR FREE BOOKS!
2 FREE NOVELS PLUS 2 FREE GIFTS!

✦ Harlequin®

ROMANTIC
SUSPENSE

Sparked by Danger, Fueled by Passion.

YES! Please send me 2 FREE Harlequin® Romantic Suspense novels and my 2 FREE gifts (gifts are worth about $10). After receiving them, if I don't wish to receive any more books, I can return the shipping statement marked "cancel." If I don't cancel, I will receive 4 brand-new novels every month and be billed just $4.49 per book in the U.S. or $5.24 per book in Canada. That's a saving of at least 14% off the cover price! It's quite a bargain! Shipping and handling is just 50¢ per book in the U.S. and 75¢ per book in Canada.* I understand that accepting the 2 free books and gifts places me under no obligation to buy anything. I can always return a shipment and cancel at any time. Even if I never buy another book, the two free books and gifts are mine to keep forever.

240/340 HDN FEFR

Name	(PLEASE PRINT)

Address	Apt. #

City	State/Prov.	Zip/Postal Code

Signature (if under 18, a parent or guardian must sign)

Mail to the **Reader Service:**

IN U.S.A.: P.O. Box 1867, Buffalo, NY 14240-1867
IN CANADA: P.O. Box 609, Fort Erie, Ontario L2A 5X3

Not valid for current subscribers to Harlequin Romantic Suspense books.

Want to try two free books from another line?
Call 1-800-873-8635 or visit www.ReaderService.com.

---

* Terms and prices subject to change without notice. Prices do not include applicable taxes. Sales tax applicable in N.Y. Canadian residents will be charged applicable taxes. Offer not valid in Quebec. This offer is limited to one order per household. All orders subject to credit approval. Credit or debit balances in a customer's account(s) may be offset by any other outstanding balance owed by or to the customer. Please allow 4 to 6 weeks for delivery. Offer available while quantities last.

Your Privacy—The Reader Service is committed to protecting your privacy. Our Privacy Policy is available online at www.ReaderService.com or upon request from the Reader Service.

We make a portion of our mailing list available to reputable third parties that offer products we believe may interest you. If you prefer that we not exchange your name with third parties, or if you wish to clarify or modify your communication preferences, please visit us at www.ReaderService.com/consumerschoice or write to us at Reader Service Preference Service, P.O. Box 9062, Buffalo, NY 14269. Include your complete name and address.

HRS11B

*Lady Priscilla and the Duke of Reighland play
a deliciously sexy game of cat and mouse in
LADY PRISCILLA'S SHAMEFUL SECRET,
the third and final installment of the Ladies in Disgrace
trilogy, a playful and provocative Regency series
by award-winning author Christine Merrill.*

He was staring at her again, thoughtfully. "Considering your pedigree, it should be advantageous to the man involved, as well. You are young, beautiful and well born. Why are you not married already, I wonder? For how could any man resist such a sweet and amenable nature?"

"Perhaps I was waiting for you, Your Grace." She dropped her smile, making no effort to hide her contempt.

"Or perhaps the rumors I hear are true and you have dishonored yourself."

"Who…" The word had escaped before she could marshal a denial. But she had experienced a moment's uncontrollable fear that, somewhere Dru had been that she had not, the ugly truth of it all had escaped. And that now, her happily married sister was laughing at her expense.

"Who told me? Why, you did, just now." He was smiling in triumph. "It is commonly known that the younger daughter of the Earl of Benbridge no longer goes about in society because of the presence of the elder. But I assumed there would be more to it than that. And I was correct."

Success at last, though it came with a sick feeling in her stomach, and the wish that it had come any way but this. She had finally managed to ruin everything. Father would be furious if this opportunity slipped through her fingers. It would serve him right, for pushing this upon her. "You have guessed correctly, Your Grace. And now, I assume that this interview is at an end." She gestured toward the door.

"On the contrary," he replied. "You have much more to tell me, before I depart from here...."

If you like your Regencies fun,
sexy and full of scandal then you'll love
LADY PRISCILLA'S SHAMEFUL SECRET
Available May 2012

Don't miss the other two titles in this outrageous trilogy:
LADY FOLBROKE'S DELICIOUS DECEPTION
LADY DRUSILLA'S ROAD TO RUIN